Operation 2

John Agnew

For Sheila … who puts up with it all.

Table of Contents

Reuters International News Agency report – August 19th 1991.

Reports have been received of a possible coup attempt in the Soviet Union.

It is reported that the Soviet Premier, Mikhail Gorbachev, is under house arrest and that several senior government ministers have been arrested.

BBC 6 o'clock News – August 23rd 1991.

"It has now been confirmed that the Soviet Premier, Mikhail Gorbachev, is dead. How he died is not yet known, only that it happened at his Dacha in the Crimea.

Reports from Moscow seem to indicate that the coup by Soviets hard-liners and members of the military has been successful in overthrowing the moderates in the government.

Other reports also state that Soviet troops are moving into Estonia, which declared itself an independent state on August the 20th …"

Reuters International News Agency report – April 3rd 1992.

The new German Chancellor has again demanded talks with Poland over a "readjustment" of the post-war borders and a return of "German territory" to the Federal Republic.

BBC 6 o'clock News – April 27th 1992.

"Talks between the German and Polish governments regarding the disputed territory in Western Poland appear to have collapsed today after the Polish delegation apparently walked out of the negotiations …"

CNN NEWS – May 16th 1992.

"Tensions appear to be growing between the Federal Republic of Germany and Poland as the dispute between the two countries over their mutual borders continues.

The Soviet Union issued a statement condemning what it said was Germany's 'unreasonable demands' and claiming that the Federal Republic's new right-wing government 'posed a threat to peace and stability' in Europe."

Extract from a confidential memo from the Polish Ministry of Foreign Affairs to the Ministry of National Defence – May 25th 1992.

"The Soviets have indicated that they are willing to support us militarily in the event of Germany using force to impose their territorial demands on us. In return for this they appear to require basing facilities for their armed forces, details of the size and disposition of these forces to be clarified during formal talks. It is possible that they may be hoping to relocate their current Group of Soviet Forces Germany when they leave Germany under the treaty. Whatever their planning it is clear that they are very concerned by a resurgent Germany and take a pessimistic view of its future policies towards Eastern Europe.

In light of the above, the Prime Minister requests a feasibility study on the defence of our Western borders in the face of a German incursion or even a full-scale invasion. Please factor in limited Soviet military support (details to follow) …"

Part 1

"Operation Thor"

Chapter 1

"War is the unfolding of miscalculations." Barbara W. Tuchman.

"If it can go wrong, it will. And at the worst possible time." Murphy's Law (incorporating O'Toole's corollary).

Güben, Federal Republic of Germany, 17:30 hrs, June 27th 1992.

Leutnant Krause stood well back from the window in a room overlooking the River Neisse and the bridge over it which spanned the border between the Federal Republic and Poland. He was hoping to observe the opposite Polish riverbank without being observed himself.

"Anything, *Feldwebel?*" he asked his platoon sergeant, who had been observing the opposite riverbank for the past hour.

"They're there, *Herr Leutnant*. There was movement behind those apartments over there." He pointed to a row of cream painted apartment blocks which sat back from the riverbank.

Krause lifted his field glasses and panned along the block. Nothing was moving now but he hadn't expected to see anything. Since the incident at the border crossing point near Frankfurt-am-Oder a fortnight earlier, German and Polish forces massing on the border were being particularly careful not to provoke another incident.

Despite the fact that this bridge was one of the few crossing points still open, traffic, both vehicular and pedestrian, was light. Civilians on both sides of the border were keeping their heads down, those that hadn't already moved out further away from the border and the two armies massing there. There was a storm coming, both sides had gone too far to back down now.

Krause scanned the far bank for a final time, taking in the sentries at the far end of the bridge and the sandbagged machine gun post covering the bridge itself. Unlike the heavy German military presence which was being very obvious, the Polish presence was very low-key.

"I don't like them not being visible," he said. "I would have expected more of a show of force." He looked at his platoon sergeant. "I think they're ready to make a move. I think they'll try to blow the bridge."

"Tonight, Sir?"

"Tonight. We'll go tonight."

Krause made his way out onto the street to pass the word to the local commander, a Captain in the Territorial forces, that the Bundeswehr engineers would remove the demolition charges secretly placed by the Polish army tonight.

On his way he passed one of the Fuchs armoured personnel carriers belonging to his engineer platoon parked up in the streets near the bridge. His regular *Heer* engineers, distinguishable from the local Territorial forces by their new-style *Flecktarn* camouflage uniforms, were resting around them in preparation for the expected increase in activity after dark.

He found Hauptmann Weiss in his "command post" in one of the local civilian's dining room. A former Major in the East German *Nationale Volksarmee*, Weiss was his usual rather cold self.

"Ah, *Leutnant*. Everything ready in case our friends try anything?"

"Yes, Sir. In fact we'll be making our move to remove the charges tonight."

"Tonight?"

Krause nodded and briefly explained his suspicions that the Poles would try to blow the bridge in the near future. "Actually it's more of a feeling, Sir," he concluded with a shrug of his shoulders.

Weiss eyed him with a cool stare.

"A … feeling, *Leutnant*? How very … interesting."

Krause wisely chose not to reply and just stood there, feeling more uncomfortable by the second. Weiss continued to look at him for several increasingly uncomfortable seconds then shrugged.

"Well, if you're sure and everything's ready … We'll play it safe and assume they'll try and blow the bridge sooner rather than later. Go and make your final preparations, *Leutnant*."

Krause saluted and made his way to brief his platoon.

Güben, Federal Republic of Germany, 01:45 hrs, June 28th 1992.

The engineer corporal eased the night vision goggles up onto his forehead and rubbed his eyes.

"Your turn," he handed the goggles to one of the two engineer privates in the room with him.

The soldier settled the goggles comfortably on his face and took up a position near the window. Several minutes later he ceased scanning from side to side and studied the area of the bridge intently for several seconds.

"I think I have something." He removed the goggles and handed them back to the corporal. "At eleven o'clock, pillar on the left, down near the waterline."

"*Ja*, they're our boys. If we didn't see them, and we're looking for them, hopefully the *Polacken* won't even know they're there."

The figures in the green glow of the night vision goggles were clearly working on one of the bridge's pillars, removing the demolition charges.

"Fetch *Feldwebel* Braun," the corporal ordered.

The private returned within minutes accompanied by both the platoon sergeant and Leutnant Krause. The corporal pointed out where the activity was taking place.

3

"Well, *Feldwebel*, the divers appear to be doing their job. So far, so good."

Without warning, seconds later, the whole area around the bridge was lit up by a burst of harsh white light as a flare rose from the East bank. It revealed a small team of divers attempting to remove demolition charges at the Polish end of the bridge. They momentarily froze then burst into frenzied activity.

"Oh, shit!" The corporal tore off the goggles, his night vision ruined by the flare overloading the image intensifier. An engineer section was caught in the glare crouching near the German end of the bridge, ready to clear the charges under the roadway itself.

No one knew who fired first although it appeared the first shot came from the German end of the bridge from one of the local Territorials. Whoever fired failed to survive the next half hour as did any witnesses. The Polish machine gun in the sandbagged position began hammering the German end of the bridge, returning fire and sending rounds into the sentries there. Shocked Territorials took cover and began to return fire.

"Orders, Sir?" The sergeant looked at Krause. None of the engineers had returned fire as of yet. Outside the amount of firing increased as a heavy machine gun began to fire.

Fuck it, thought Krause. *It's already an international incident.* "Open fire! Target the machine gun post!"

Tracer rounds reached out towards the German demolition team from one of the buildings on the Polish side of the river. All around heavy firing was sending rounds at both sides' troops and also beyond either end of the bridge, tearing into buildings still occupied by both sides' civilians.

One of the engineers' Fuchs APCs moved up towards the bridge end, its machine gun hosing tracer towards the Polish machine gun, covering the withdrawal of the surviving Territorials pinned down at the bridge. On the opposite bank the bow of a BMP fighting vehicle nosed into view from the park facing the bridge. The BMP fired as the flare began to burn out and the 73mm round tore into the Fuchs' driver's compartment. A burst of flame blew over the rear of the APC as smoke began to pour from it. Neither the driver nor the machine gunner made it out.

Further flares from both sides burst in the night sky and by their light several rounds from hand-held anti-tank weapons flew towards the BMP. Two of them impacted on the vehicle's bow and its crew scrambled clear as it began to burn. Shortly afterwards its ammunition detonated, the vehicle rocking from internal explosions amid the cracking of small-arms rounds cooking off.

Ten minutes after the fighting began, someone decided to fire an RPG in the direction of the demolition team in the water. Most of them had already become casualties but the three survivors followed them as the HEAT round detonated the demolition charges they had removed. The resulting massive explosion wrecked the Polish end of the bridge and killed the machine gun crew in the sandbagged position.

The sudden shock of the detonation forced a pause in the fighting. The firing died away as officers and NCOs on both sides gained control of their men. Eventually a calm fell on the area around the bridge and the darkness returned as the flares burned out to be replaced by the flickering light from the burning armoured vehicles.

After an hour Hauptmann Weiss had contacted and come to an agreement with the Polish commander to allow civilian ambulances on both sides to evacuate the wounded, both military and civilian, of which there were several dozen. After that both sides began to gather up their dead.

As things quietened down in Güben, in local military headquarters and in the respective capitals' seats of power, plans were put in motion. Once again the ambitions of politicians led them to miscalculate and their actions would bring unforeseen consequences. For the third time in the Twentieth Century Europe was slipping into war.

Chapter 2

June 29th – July 5th 1992.

The first deliberate shots of the German-Polish confrontation were fired by a battalion of M109 155mm self-propelled guns of the 13th Panzer Division at 11:00 hrs on June 29th. The shells fell on the concentration area of a Motor Rifle battalion belonging to 2nd Motor Rifle Division. Casualties among the sleeping troops were heavy.

Within 30 minutes artillery fire from the Polish Division was falling on 13th Panzer Division units. Within an hour 8th Panzergrenadier Division's and 4th Motor Rifle Division's artillery had joined in. The fire and counter-battery fire continued during the course of the day, falling off after several hours as surviving units moved position or moved up to their jumping-off positions in the case of the German forces.

Just before first light a flight of two Luftwaffe Phantoms fired anti-radiation missiles at an anti-aircraft missile battery east of Lebus. Severe damage was done to the air-defence unit and it was followed by the destruction or suppression of several more units, creating a gap in the air defences of that sector.

Further air strikes followed on Polish army units in position near crossing points over the River Oder selected by German IV Corps for assault river crossings. By first light the air strikes had been superseded by artillery fire interdicting the approaches to the selected crossing points. By mid-morning the crossings were in progress and German engineers were building bridges under an air defence umbrella which was fighting off the first attacks by the Polish Air Force.

Most of the Bundeswehr's IV Corps was made up of ex-East German Volksarmee personnel with a leavening of Bundeswehr regulars. Much of the equipment was also ex-Volksarmee pending disposal and replacement by West German equipment. In western Poland the same types of tanks and AFVs used by both sides, clashed.

The Polish Republic, 15km East of the Oder River, 11:45 hrs, July 1st 1992.

The leading 13th Panzer Division T-72 nosed past the burning Luchs armoured reconnaissance vehicle. In the treeline 500 metres to the front the T-55 which killed it also burned. The Polish 2nd Motor Rifle Division may have been falling back but they still had teeth.

Despite over a year's integration into the Bundeswehr and intensive training in Western tactics, under the pressure of combat conditions some units reverted to the familiar, and less complex, Warsaw Pact tactics. In this case the first platoon was moving while a second provided covering fire from overwatch. To their front the first smoke shells were impacting on the treeline.

Once the smokescreen had thickened an extended line of BMP armoured fighting vehicles raced forward spraying the treeline with co-axial machine gun fire. The vehicles halted, Panzergrenadiers poured out and assaulted the suspected enemy position. As the lack of enemy defensive fire had already indicated, the Poles were long gone. The dismounts quickly re-embarked and the German advance rolled on.

Five kilometres further east the Poles temporarily stopped running.

Overconfidence was beginning to set in among some of the pursuing German units, sometimes with fatal consequences. Several tanks were left burning in the fields surrounding the village of Kowalow, destroyed by the defenders of this important road junction. It was clear the Polish forces were determined to make the Germans pay for taking the road junction and cutting the railway line.

It took an hour to launch the first hasty attack on the village. Under cover of a barrage a Panzergrenadier battalion, supported by a tank company, assaulted from the southwest with a company either side of the main road and another following up in reserve. It met with limited success.

Anti-tank missiles in the small wood west of the village destroyed the left flank platoon before being silenced by the German battalion's heavy mortar company. More missile teams concealed in the undergrowth between the railway line and the village itself caused further casualties to the right flank company before smoke shells concealed the attackers.

After dismounting, the infantry managed to fight their way across the railway line but were halted amongst the houses on the village's outskirts. Throwing in the reserve company helped to secure the first houses but they were unable to make further progress. Fighting died away during a sudden thunderstorm which soaked the village, helping to dampen down some scattered fires, both burning houses and vehicles.

A second assault, attempting to flank the village from the east, suffered heavy casualties to tank fire from the woods around Maniszewo to their east. Again the attack died away in house-to-house fighting on the edge of the village. By now the delay had resulted in an uncomfortable discussion between the Brigade commander and the Divisional commander which included a full and frank discussion on the importance of sticking to the timetable of the advance.

It took a sustained artillery barrage which reduced most of Kowalow to rubble, killing many of the Polish defenders and a few Polish civilians who had refused to evacuate, to soften up the defenders enough for fresh German troops to finally capture the village. This escalation of the level of violence turned what had begun as a limited action designed to bring Poland to the negotiating table into something much darker. The bitterness caused by this and similar incidents would make any attempts to resolve the conflict by the UN almost impossible. Already events were slipping out of the politicians' control.

Although Kowalow was taken, the vital road junction was blocked by rubble which would take several hours to clear. In addition heavy casualties had been caused to 33rd Panzergrenadier Brigade causing the Divisional commander to halt its advance pending reorganisation. Another brigade from reserve was brought forward to take over the advance but the German advance had been delayed by several hours.

International condemnation of the German incursion into Poland was swift and loud. Even Germany's NATO allies publicly expressed their concern regarding the German-Polish build-up and, after the invasion, privately were appalled at Germany's actions. A crisis meeting at the UN resulted in the Security Council calling for an immediate ceasefire and cessation of hostilities.

As the fighting entered its third day, on July 2nd, the Soviets announced that they would take action to end the fighting and, as they put it, "restore order in Central Europe". To do this they intended to use the Group of Soviet Forces Germany to close German supply lines and prevent the means to continue the push into Poland from reaching German forces.

Despite their opposition to German actions, NATO felt it extremely unwise to allow Soviet forces free range within Germany. NATO announced that its forces would move up to the former Inner German Border but take no further action unless Soviet forces crossed the former IGB. In effect they occupied their planned Cold War General Deployment Positions which had been designed to be occupied in the run up to any potential invasion of West Germany by the Warsaw Pact.

Late on July 2nd GSFG units left their barracks and began to take up positions blocking German supply lines by occupying vital road junctions, blocking railway lines and taking control of important bridges. Other units sealed off the former IGB. Overnight there were clashes between Soviet units and German logistic units, fortunately without bloodshed at this point.

On July 3rd, after an intense 24 hours of heated debate, NATO came to an agreement that further action was necessary. Despite reservations by some of its members, particularly Greece and Italy, the situation in Central Europe was felt to be serious enough to threaten a wider conflict and NATO began to mobilise as a precaution. However, there was firm agreement that there would be no political, and under no circumstances any military, support for Germany's actions against Poland.

The setback at Kowalow and other similar blocking actions by Polish forces had slowed the German advance. By July 3rd Polish resistance had hardened and mounting losses amongst German forces, both due to battlefield casualties amongst men and machines and increasing mechanical breakdowns of armoured vehicles, had resulted in the German advance coming to a virtual halt. The result was a salient stretching 30km deep and 20km wide into Poland east of the Oder either side of Frankfurt an der Oder.

After two days of small-scale attacks and counterattacks which barely moved the static front, coupled with the Russian blockade, IV (GE) Corps was beginning to run short of vital supplies. Attempts to open negotiations at the UN by the Polish government had been ignored by the German government up to this point but a realisation that things were no longer going their way resulted in an expressed interest in opening talks.

However, in an attempt to influence any negotiations, fresh German forces from I (GE) Corps in Lower Saxony began to move eastwards towards the IGB on 5th July. This was also partly in response to reports that Soviet forces based in the western Soviet Union had begun to move into eastern Poland.

15km East of the Oder River, Poland, July 5th 1992.

The commander of the tank company guarding the crossroads hunched miserably standing in the turret of his T-55 in the drizzle watching a retreating army. The growing lack of fuel and ammunition had made it increasingly difficult for IV (GE) Corps to hold against increasing Polish counterattacks. Eventually German troops were forced to give ground and by first light were in flight. A disciplined retreat but a retreat just the same.

A steady stream of supply units, most of them with empty vehicles, medical units and repair units moving westwards had been replaced by artillery and air-defence units. Next would come combat units and behind them, the Polish army.

An hour later battered armoured and Panzergreandier units were pouring past. Many of the vehicles showing visible signs of damage and even a few having to be towed by other armoured vehicles. The sound of gunfire could be heard, growing louder as it came closer. It wasn't long before the last reconnaissance forces in contact with the enemy headed past the rearguard, moving fast.

They were barely out of sight when Polish helicopter gunships appeared, hovering over the forest in the near distance. Two flew towards the German positions and were engaged by a concealed Gepard self-propelled anti-aircraft vehicle. Its twin 35mm cannon shells blowing pieces of fuselage and engine away and causing the wreckage to plunge to earth. The surviving Mi-24 "Hind" launched an anti-tank missile at the Gepard which missed as the helicopter was forced to take evasive action to avoid return fire from the German vehicle.

Artillery fire began impacting on suspected German positions, causing a steady drain of casualties to the dug-in infantry and damaging the optics and running gear of armoured vehicles. After a few minutes the high explosive was replaced by smoke shells as Polish armoured forces began the ground assault.

A Motor Rifle battalion supported by a tank company raced forward, attempting to overrun the defenders before they could recover from the artillery barrage or pull back. Neither side possessed thermal imaging devices on the vehicles involved which would allow them to fire through the smokescreen with any chance of causing casualties to their opponents. The result of this was a short-ranged melee when the Poles reached the German positions.

BMPs halted and Motor Riflemen poured out to assault the dug-in Panzergrenadiers as the smokescreen began to fade. The empty BMPs began to use their 73mm cannon and co-axial machine guns to suppress the German trenches as Riflemen charged forward firing their assault rifles on the move and grenading trenches. At such close range both attackers and defenders suffered heavily. Both sides' tanks fired at what amounted to point blank range and T-55s, used by both sides, burned throughout the position.

The attacking battalion was fought to a standstill but the bloodied defenders were forced to pull back. As they retreated the Polish Hinds returned and began to pick off the retreating vehicles with their anti-tank missiles and rotary 12.7mm heavy machine guns. One of the first to go was the surviving Gepard, gutted by an AT-6 "Spiral" wire-guided missile. As the surviving hand-held anti-air missile teams were mounted in their retreating vehicles the helicopters had full reign until the rearguard survivors reached the next blocking position and its anti-aircraft cover.

Fresh Polish forces moved forward to continue the advance and assault the next German position leaving the weakened assaulting unit to mop-up and reorganise. Ambulances were quickly brought up as any German survivors left behind seemed disinclined to fight on once overrun and the wounded of both sides taken back to field hospitals. A handful of dispirited prisoners were also hustled away to rapidly-filling temporary holding camps.

Meanwhile the German retreat went on.

Chapter 3

" ... To sum up. Should the Federal Republic take this dispute with Poland further, and if military action takes place, we must be prepared to stand by our mutual assistance pact and provide military support for Polish forces if requested.

Germany's allies appear to be as worried by her right-wing drift and territorial demands as we are and would try to avoid being drawn into what they see as a German-Polish border dispute. Several NATO countries have already indicated that, unless military action takes place near the former Inner German border, they would be reluctant to support the Germans.

Should some sort of armed confrontation take place, the mere presence of Group of Soviet Forces Germany units in what would be the German rear areas and across their supply lines may be enough to prevent any large-scale German action. Should more decisive action be needed to keep the peace and stabilise the situation, which the United States has indicated they would not object to, GSFG units will be at full readiness to take limited offensive action.

Should they be needed, we will have at our disposal; 11 Tank and 8 Motor Rifle Divisions in GSFG, 2 further divisions "on exercise" in Poland and 5 Tank and 5 Motor Rifle Divisions of the Polish Army. A further 2 Tank and 2 Motor Rifle Divisions will be on alert in Byelorussia should any unforeseen emergencies occur. The Airborne forces will be placed on full alert.

Political means will be used to gain the support of the United Nations and keep NATO out of any military confrontation. The latter is already reluctant to interfere as many Western European nations share our disquiet at the increasingly aggressive and right-wing policies of the new Germany. For this reason, and for the sake of the improved relations between ourselves and the West, they will be reluctant to be seen supporting German aggression.

A strong response to the situation on our part might also bring us great advantage at home by stabilising the internal situation. A perceived external threat, especially one recalling the days of the Great Patriotic War, may kindle the patriotism of the people, rallying them behind us, and prove to certain secession-minded Republics that it is much better and safer to belong to a strong Soviet Union.

One more important point must be made, however, which may prove of interest. Defence cuts in the armed forces of NATO mean that, if the situation escalates and conflict with NATO forces becomes inevitable, it may be to our advantage to make the most of any situation which arises and neutralise Germany completely ... "

Extract from a confidential memo to the Soviet Ruling Army Council written by Marshal Kalugin on the developing situation on the German-Polish border dated, June 18th 1992.

East of the former IGB, Federal Republic of Germany, 03:00 hrs, July 6th 1992.

The commander of the Luchs armoured car belonging to 3rd Panzer Division's 3rd Reconnaissance Battalion watched the Soviet outpost through the vehicle's night vision sight. Two squads of Russian infantry had erected a temporary barrier of razor wire at the minor crossroads and were manning a vehicle checkpoint. Their two BTR armoured personnel carriers were parked in a position to cover any vehicles approaching the crossroads.

In the East the fighting between German and Polish forces had reached a crisis point. Chronically short of ammunition and fuel the forces of IV (GE) Corps had been driven back almost to the River Oder in disarray the previous day. As a result the German Army was making a determined attempt to re-supply IV Corps and halt the Poles before the confrontation grew into a wider war. This involved attempts by units of I and III (GE) Corps in Western Germany to break the Soviet blockade, using force if necessary.

Through the night sight the Luchs commander saw the German infantry, who had managed to infiltrate close to the checkpoint without being spotted by the bored guards, make their move. The infantry raced forward and quickly disarmed the sentries, forcing them to lie on the road. At the same time other troops threw stun grenades into the back of the APCs, rounding up the disorientated soldiers who had been asleep in the passenger compartment as they staggered out.

Once the barriers had been removed from the road the reconnaissance unit passed the word back to the waiting supply column. Within minutes a platoon of tanks were clattering past the humiliated Russians sitting lined up along the roadside with their hands on their heads under guard. Behind the tanks came the infantry fighting vehicles and behind them the supply convoy. They headed for the next Soviet roadblock, hoping once again to neutralise it without bloodshed.

10 km east of the former IGB, near Klötze, Federal Republic of Germany, 03:30 hrs, July 6th 1992.

To the south of 3rd Panzer Division, 1st Panzer Division was also sending supply convoys eastwards. They were also probing through the darkness, avoiding Soviet blocking positions where they could and seizing them where they could not. Inevitably the good luck that had characterised the early stages of the operation ran out.

The 1st Panzer Division Luchs had barely got into position to observe the suspected Russian checkpoint before a 125mm round from the concealed T-80 struck the driver's position. There was a bright flash as the armour-piercing round smashed its way through the driver's compartment, through the driver and along the length of the vehicle to bury itself in the engine block at the rear.

The vehicle began to burn and ammunition crackled as it cooked off in the turret. No-one got out. The idea of a bloodless operation died with its crew. The Russians had drawn first blood and demonstrated their determination to halt the German-Polish fighting by any means necessary.

Behind the leading reconnaissance element a tank platoon eased into position to engage the Soviet tanks. The T-80 which had killed the Luchs was the first to be destroyed, a Leopard 2 sending a 120mm round into its hull. A short firefight saw the Leopards knock out the remaining two T-80s of the Russian platoon followed by a hasty infantry assault on the Russian position.

The German Panzergrenadiers cleared the Russian infantry from the checkpoint after a short, sharp action but were caught themselves by a sudden counterattack while reorganising. An unexpected mortar salvo bracketed the former Soviet position causing casualties amongst the regrouping Germans and was followed by a strong infantry assault in company strength supported by the heavy machine guns of their accompanying BTR APCs.

The Russian assault was halted due to the German tank support but the German supply effort was also stopped in its tracks. Both sides had suffered casualties but were unwilling, at this point at least, to escalate the confrontation. On both sides reports were being studied by the chain of command and there was a pause for directions from the respective governments. Meanwhile on the eastern borders of Germany the German-Polish fighting raged on.

East of the former IGB, near Klötze, Federal Republic of Germany, 17:00 hrs, July 6th 1992.

The lead German battlegroup of 1st Panzer Division had dug-in short of the former Soviet position to avoid the pre-registered mortar fire which had harassed them intermittently during the afternoon. The accompanying supply vehicles were dispersed in hides for safety although the chances of them completing their re-supply mission were slim.

The first the Germans knew of political decisions made in Moscow was a sudden barrage of 120mm heavy mortar bombs landing on their positions. Within minutes their outposts in front of their positions reported tank and Motor Rifle forces in battalion strength advancing towards their positions before falling back through the main position.

Milan anti-tank missiles made the first kills as the Russian vehicles entered their range. Two T-80s were left burning as the attackers rolled on. Closer to the German positions the Leopard platoon joined in with their 120mm cannon causing further casualties to the enemy armoured vehicles.

16

The German infantry were suffering under the mortar barrage but not as much as if the Soviets had followed their normal doctrine and hammered them with artillery. A political decision had been made to avoid using heavy artillery so as to avoid damage to property and civilian casualties in what was a still peaceful countryside. As far as the Russian military was concerned they were fighting with one hand tied behind their back. The Soviets had no military manuals covering "hearts and minds" operations but it did have several extolling the virtues of saturating their opponents in high explosives prior to an assault.

The Russian tanks slowed and commenced firing on the move as the BTRs halted and the infantry began to dismount. As the Motor Riflemen began their assault the volume of fire from the German positions began to slacken. As they advanced the Russians watched as the Panzergrenadiers began to withdraw and board their Marder Infantry Fighting Vehicles.

The sudden German retreat was as a result of orders passed down from the Chancellor's office to avoid further confrontation with Soviet forces. One armed conflict at a time was felt to be enough. The Bundeswehr forces managed to disengage cleanly and pulled back, closely followed by Soviet forces.

North of Wolfsburg, Federal Republic of Germany, 03:00 hrs, July 7th 1992.

Corporal Eldon listened to the sound of gunfire coming from the northeast. It appeared to be moving closer to his position. He kept his eye glued to the Image Intensifier sight of his Scimitar reconnaissance vehicle. He had been briefed on the developing situation between the Bundeswehr and GSFG forces and, along with the rest of the 13/18 Hussars Armoured Reconnaissance Regiment in the British Army of the Rhine's Covering Force, was monitoring the situation as sporadic fighting moved westwards towards the IGB.

Not far away units of the Bundeswehr's 1st Panzer Division, having failed in their mission to push supplies to the beleaguered IV (GE) Corps on the Oder, were withdrawing in the face of pressure from the Soviet GSFG forces. Casualties, so far, had been low on both sides but the Russians had made it clear that might no longer be the case if the Germans failed to pull back to the former IGB.

"Want me to spell you, Corporal?" asked Trooper Grainger from the commander's seat normally occupied by Corporal Eldon.

"Yeah," Eldon's eyes were tiring after staring at the fuzzy green phosphor image created by the Image Intensifier for about 30 minutes. "Let's change."

The pair awkwardly manoeuvred themselves to change seats within the cramped confines of the turret. Grainger, with his eyes now glued to the sight, and Eldon, rubbing his closed eyes, resumed their vigil as small-arms fire crackled in the distance, punctuated occasionally by tank gunfire. The sound of fighting was getting closer to the sector covered by British forces.

"I have movement," Grainger announced. "Quarter left, one thousand metres, heavy vehicles."

Eldon keyed his microphone to report to the Troop leader. "India One One, this is India One One Alpha. Contact. Wait. Out."

Eldon stood up in his hatch and peered into the darkness. "Talk to me, Grainger."

"Large vehicles … tanks … Leopards, I think."

Eldon could hear the sounds of heavy diesels coming from the direction of the vehicles but darkness still hid them from his view. "They're well out of their sector if it's the Box Heads and if it's not then the shit's about to hit the fan."

Even as he spoke the smelly stuff hit the proverbial cooling instrument. A glowing blob connected with the rear of one of the retreating tanks followed by a bright flash as the armour-piercing round penetrated the tank's engine block.

"Jesus!" Grainger's sight flared at the explosion, temporarily ruining his night vision.

In the glare of the explosion Eldon glimpsed another two tanks, identified as Leopards by their blocky turrets, with their turrets and main guns pointed to their rear covering a pursuing enemy. Both tanks fired past their burning companion as the crew of the stricken tank clambered out. Further away there was another explosion as their attacker paid the price. The two Leopards quickly moved off, disappearing into the darkness, heading west.

"Hello, India One One, this is India One One Alpha. Two Heer Leopards heading west nine hundred metres northeast of my position. A third Leopard has been hit and is now burning. The friendlies have returned fire and an unknown vehicles is now also burning. Out."

"Understood, One One Alpha. Continue to observe. Out."

"More vehicles … near the burning Leopard," Grainger reported. "Can't get a positive id but they definitely look like Ivans."

"India One One, India One One Alpha. More vehicles, number unknown, in vicinity of burning friendly. Unidentified at present, possibly Soviet. Out."

Eldon was still peering into the darkness, trying to catch a glimpse of the possible Russian vehicles, when a muzzle flash lit the night with a crack. A glowing tracer ended in another blinding flash of light off to Eldon's left and seconds later another vehicle was burning.

"Fucking Hell!" Where did that one go?" asked Grainger, pulling his face back from the sight in surprise.

Eldon was turned towards the latest blazing vehicle. He was afraid he knew the identity of the latest victim. His Troop Sergeant's Scimitar was stationed somewhere in that direction and he doubted any other vehicles was near. Beneath him the turret traversed slowly as Grainger held the advancing vehicles in his sights.

"Hello, India One One Alpha, this is India One One. Sitrep, Over."

19

"India One One Alpha. The unidentified vehicles are continuing west. They have engaged and destroyed an unidentified target three hundred metres at my nine o'clock," Eldon paused for a second. "Believe target may have been India One One Bravo. Out."

"India One One. Understood, Out."

"Fuck me! You reckon that was Sergeant Armstrong's wagon? Did anybody get out?" Grainger asked.

"Dunno. Doubt it, it went up straight away."

For the first time since the action started the driver, Trooper Sanderson, made his presence known.

"Are you sure it's One One Bravo? Has anybody checked?"

Eldon listened to the Troop Leader trying to contact his Sergeant on the Troop net. The silence told its own story.

"Looks like it, Sandy. Lieutenant Groves isn't getting any answer from One One Bravo."

There were further cracks of tank cannon fire from the direction the Germans and their pursuers had taken. Nearby the only sound was the popping noise of small-arms rounds being detonated by the fires and the crackle of flames as three vehicles belonging to three different armies burned. The flames threatening to be the forerunners of a much bigger blaze, one that would engulf most of Central Europe.

Chapter 4

Sergeant Armstrong and his crew were not the only NATO non-belligerents who became victims of the ongoing hostilities in Eastern Germany and along the IGB. During the confused night action on the 6/7th July along the IGB in which the Soviets repulsed all German attempts to push supplies through to the embattled IV (GE) Corps, there were several incidents in which NATO forces were fired on by Soviet forces.

Several reconnaissance vehicles of the Covering Force forward of British 1st Armoured Division were destroyed along with most of their crews by units of the Soviet 10th Guards Tank Division. Further south, in the Central Army Group sector, units of the US 3rd Armored Division were fired on and suffered casualties during a confused engagement between 12th Panzer Division and the Soviet 79th Motor Rifle Division.

The GSFG command had regained control over their forces and all Soviet units were east of the IGB by daylight on 7th July. The Politburo was in emergency session and ambassadors to the UK and US conveyed apologies to the respective governments. Urgent talks were also under way at the UN. Further hostilities were avoided, at least for the present. Neither side wanted war, or at least not a war started by accident. However, in the Kremlin, plans and contingency plans were being discussed and alerts being sent to Soviet forces in Central Europe and the Western Soviet Union.

By July 7th IV (GE) Corps had been pushed back across the River Oder. Polish forces had followed up, capturing several engineer bridges erected by the Germans and using them to cross into Germany. Supplies of fuel and ammunition had become critically low despite the retreat bringing German units closer to supply dumps situated near the west bank of the Oder.

The German ambassador to the UN and a negotiating team sent by the German Parliament were frantically trying to negotiate a ceasefire with the Polish authorities. Neither the Polish government nor the Polish Army were inclined to oblige them, particularly as the fighting had moved from Polish to German territory.

While the talks were in progress the fighting had died down as German forces were ordered to hold their position but not mount any counterattacks. In reply the Poles had halted their advance, as much to reorganise their forces as to support the peace talks. Both sides were still carrying out close air support airstrikes but the use of artillery had almost ceased.

Northeast of Mulrose, Federal Republic of Germany, 07:00 hrs, July 8th 1992.

Leutnant Krause's engineer platoon were busy preparing a minor bridge for demolition. Their escort, a much-reduced infantry platoon from 8th Panzergrenadier Division, was dug-in around the approaches to the bridge and a steady trickle of German civilians, mostly in vehicles but a few on foot, crossed heading westwards away from the fighting.

Bridges, bridges, always fucking bridges, thought Krause as he checked on his men's progress.

"Are we on track, *Feldwebel?*" he asked his Platoon Sergeant.

"Almost there, *Herr Leutnant*," replied Braun, rubbing a hand across the stubble on his chin. "Another fifteen minutes, maybe."

"Good … good," Krause felt exhausted after almost 24 hours without sleep. He looked at his Sergeant with his two-day growth of beard and red-rimmed eyes and wondered if he looked as shit as Braun did.

"Vehicles coming!" shouted one of the infantry NCOs as refugees scattered and civilian vehicles were forced into the side of the road. A motley group of armoured vehicles rumbled towards the bridge, a BMP IFV followed by three M113s with a T-55 tank bringing up the rear.

One of the M113s pulled up after crossing the bridge as the other vehicles carried on. The rear ramp dropped and an officer stepped down looking around for the man in charge of the engineers. Krause jogged over towards him and saluted the figure when he was close enough to see the badges of rank.

"*Leutnant* Krause, 2nd Company, 82nd Independent Engineer Battalion, *Herr Hauptmann.*"

The grimy Captain returned the salute wearily and glanced at the work taking place on the bridge. As he opened his mouth to speak the sound of artillery fire began from further back along the road. He looked briefly in the direction he had come before turning back to the engineer officer.

"It's started. We received word half an hour ago that the UN talks had failed. The fucking Poles are going to keep on coming and there's fuck all we can do to stop them." He paused to let Krause catch up. "*Hauptmann* Reitmann, commanding the 801st Panzergrenadier Battalion … or what's left of it. The rest of the battalion is further back up the road," he thumbed back towards the direction of the artillery fire. The faint sound of tank and small-arms fire could also now be heard.

"That's about a couple of reinforced companies and a couple of tank platoons," he said bleakly. "They'll be disengaging within the next twenty minutes … if they last that long. I hope you're ready to blow the bridge by then."

"*Feldwebel* Braun, how long?" shouted Krause.

"Five minutes, *Herr Leutnant!*" Braun replied.

"Good, *Leutnant*. Right, carry on and get your men ready to pull out. I've got another delaying position to set up." With that he returned Krause's salute and reboarded the APC which took off down the road.

For the next few minutes there was frantic activity as the demolition preparations were completed and the engineers and their infantry escort boarded their vehicles and prepared to move out.

"All ready, *Herr Leutnant*," Braun reported.

Krause was watching the road in the distance where he could see vehicles approaching at speed.

"Looks like it's time to go, *Feldwebel*." The approaching vehicles became identifiable as German BMPs. As they sped past Krause counted fifteen of them, most of them showing battle damage. He reckoned that the two reinforced companies had now been reduced to just one reinforced company.

Close behind the panzergrenadiers were four T-55 tanks. As Krause watched the rearmost tank halted with its turret turned to the rear over the engine deck and fired back down the road before continuing forward and over the bridge. One of the other tanks briefly halted and the commander shouted from the turret.

"We're the last! Blow it now!"

As the tank sped on down the road, Krause waved his platoon to follow them. The Fuchs and escorting BMPs also sped off as the demolition team prepared to blow the bridge. Krause studied the bridge approaches using his field glasses as one of his corporals knelt poised to detonate the charges. Polish tanks were now visible advancing steadily towards his position. He turned to the waiting demolition team.

"Now! Blow it now!"

The corporal pressed the switch and the bridge disappeared in smoke and flames as the charges detonated and the remains of the structure collapsed into the riverbed. Krause and his team boarded their Fuchs and roared off followed by scattered long-range machine gun fire. Behind them the lead Polish forces radioed for their own engineers to come forward. They were getting rather a lot of practice at bridge building.

Deprived of the means to defend themselves or manoeuvre against their opponents, and closely pursued by the confident Polish 3rd Army, IV(GE) Corps began to disintegrate over the course of the 8th and 9th of July. Most of the units surrendered to Polish forces or Russian units which blocked their escape westwards. However, some units or individual groups of German soldiers, mostly original Bundeswehr units, tried to disappear into the countryside. Many of these troops were convinced that the Russian intervention meant that the conflict was likely to widen.

West of Limsdorf, Federal Republic of Germany, 17:00 hrs, 9th July 1992.

Leutnant Krause's motley command was gathered in a heavily-wooded area on the fringe of a Naturepark. Apart from his reduced engineer platoon he had "acquired", mostly by accident, various waifs and strays. A pair of M113s and their panzergrenadier squads, a supply lorry and its driver, along with his small load of ammunition, an M113 armoured ambulance complete with crew and two medics and even a solitary T-55 MBT.

Half an hour ago he had watched a supply platoon surrender to Polish forces in Limsdorf. The Germans had slouched past their captors, adding their weapons and webbing to the discarded pile at the roadside and suffering the indignity of Polish troops searching them and taking the opportunity to "liberate" wallets, watches, field glasses and anything else they fancied. Most of the Germans stood sullen and apprehensive with their hands on their heads although a few looked relieved and almost happy to throw down their weapons.

After a while the prisoners were herded onto their own lorries and driven off, presumably to the hastily organised POW cages, for how long nobody knew. Shaking his head in disgust, Krause melted back into the undergrowth, determined that he and his men would not give up so easily.

Krause had decided to lay up in the heavily-wooded area. From there they could either try and evade westwards or wait and see what would happen. He suspected the fighting was not yet over and might even spread, involving NATO. If that happened they could make themselves useful as partisans causing disruption to the enemy supply lines.

The stragglers he had picked up and his own engineers were in agreement with him. Any who weren't had not accompanied them this far, being cut loose along the way. Most of those remaining had all served in the former West German Army, the majority of IV Corps being former East German *Volksarmee* troops, most of whom it now appeared were unenthusiastic about the Polish venture from the start, or at least now they were losing.

He knew that most of the vehicles would have to be abandoned eventually, either through mechanical breakdown, lack of fuel or too difficult to conceal. The tank would have to go first but for the moment they would be useful to ferry his small force as far from enemy forces as possible.

Soon the small convoy headed off, further into the Naturepark. Only one of many similar groups with the same idea, melting into any suitable concealing terrain and waiting for the chance to strike back.

The German Army lost over 39000 men, just over 30000 as prisoners of war, and over 1100 armoured vehicles destroyed or captured during the ill-fated Polish invasion. However, around 4000 men and 100 armoured vehicles, mostly from 9th Panzergrenadier Division, managed to escape captivity and conceal themselves in the eastern German countryside. The Polish Army was able to make good much of its losses in vehicles and equipment from captured German stocks.

The shock and humiliation of their defeat forced the German government to agree to a ceasefire. Flush with victory the Polish magnanimously ceased their stalling of the negotiations. However, further negotiations were hampered by the Germans' refusal to come to any long-term agreement on their differences with Poland while Soviet and Polish troops remained on German soil. The loss of IV (GE) Corps was a major blow to German national pride and they were in no mood to appear weak or to compromise. On the other hand both the Soviets and Poles refused to back down while German demands became more strident and there was no settlement on German claims to Polish territory.

Tensions in Europe continued to be high with NATO almost fully mobilised and Soviet forces in Germany and Poland on full alert. Forces in the Western Soviet Union were also mobilising. Governments throughout Western Europe were contemplating the very thing that the end of the Cold War had seemed to release them from, the threat of a major war in Europe.

Part 2

"Operation Zhukov"

Chapter 5

In the aftermath of the German-Polish ceasefire, and in the face of the recalcitrance of the German government, the Soviets quickly realised that the Polish dispute was not resolved. Despite their defeat the Germans were as stubborn as ever and it became clear that their national pride had suffered a severe blow and that they would take steps to restore their pride and those steps would lead to more conflict.

The Soviets had always believed that German reunification was a major mistake and that a reunited Germany was a threat to peace in Europe. The events of June 28th to July 9th only confirmed the Russian's fears and also the fears of East European countries as well as several Western European countries.

After much internal debate on July 11th-12th the Soviet Politburo decided that they must take steps to neutralise Germany, preventing them from destabilising Europe and being a threat to the Soviets themselves. If military action was necessary then this was the time to press their advantage. Germany was on the back foot over its defeat in Poland and their NATO allies were disturbed by their aggression against Poland and lukewarm in their support.

An old Cold War plan for an assault on West Germany had been dusted off and hurriedly updated when fighting commenced in Poland. Soviet forces now received their orders for large-scale military operations in Germany.

The aims of the plan, codenamed "Operation Zhukov", were to neutralise the German army, capture key areas of German territory to be used as bargaining counters in subsequent negotiations and bring down the current German government. If Germany was forced to leave NATO it would be even better but was not regarded as essential.

The Soviet army was given four days to capture, or bring within artillery range to threaten them, their objectives – Hamburg, The Ruhr and Frankfurt. It was also to defeat the Bundeswehr in battle and destroy or severely damage the German military machine and its ability to wage war.

The aims of the Soviet actions were to be explained to NATO through diplomatic channels and conflict with NATO forces was to be avoided if possible. However, military action against NATO troops was authorised if required. It soon became clear to the Politburo, and had been admitted by the Soviet military from the outset, that NATO forces would have to be engaged from the outset and the Soviet leadership became resigned to the fact that the war would widen. They felt that the neutralisation of Germany would be worth the risk of even a limited war with NATO.

The original plan envisioned only using Soviet Category 1 formations but the inevitable involvement of NATO resulted in a re-appraisal. This resulted in Category 2 Divisions beginning to mobilise although a decision was made that only the Category 1 Divisions would be used initially. Pessimists in the Stavka fully expected that more forces would be needed at some point.

Operation Zhukov itself was the overall plan for the incursion into Western Germany (the term "invasion" was studiously avoided). In retrospect one of its main drawbacks was that it was a version of an earlier Warsaw Pact plan for a limited war with NATO and was originally designed for larger forces, particularly the participation of the Nationale Volksarmee, the NVA, the former East German Army. The reduced number of available units was to prove a major handicap to the Soviets taking their objectives and was to have serious repercussions.

Zhukov itself was divided into four subordinate operations:-

"Operation Kursk" was 2nd Guards Army's operations around Hamburg and Lower Saxony. An airborne assault was to be made on Hamburg Airport to either allow reinforcements to be flown in or to cause disruption in the city itself. Another, smaller, airborne assault was to be made on Bremen to disrupt supplies to US forces in Southern Germany which mostly came through the port of Bremerhaven.

Units of 2nd Guards Army were tasked with bypassing Hamburg to the north, cutting the city off from the Baltic coast and NATO forces from Denmark. Further divisions were to advance westwards to Bremen with some proceeding southwest to the Dutch border, cutting off NATO's Northern Army Group from easy access to the North Sea ports, while another division moved south to Bielfeld to cut off I (GE) and I (BR) Corps and join with other Soviet forces from 3rd Shock Army.

"Operation Konev" was 3rd Shock Army's operations against the Ruhr. Airborne diversionary attacks on Hannover were designed to cause disruption and an attack on Hameln aimed to capture the bridges over the Weser. The main effort of 3rd Shock Army was an attempt to encircle the Ruhr by breaking through the sector held by the Belgian I (BE) Corps.

"Operation Minsk" was 8th Guards Army's operations to punch through the Americans in the area of the Fulda Gap and quickly advance southwestwards to cross the Rhine at Koblenz using bridges captured by yet another Airborne assault. Units would then advance northwards up the west bank of the Rhine to Cologne and complete the encirclement of the Ruhr. Other divisions would advance southwest and encircle Frankfurt.

"Operation Berlin" envisaged diversionary attacks by 1st Guards Tank Army to tie up elements of VII (US) Corps and prevent them interfering in the assault on Frankfurt by counterattacking in support of V (US) Corps. Airborne operations would take bridges around Mannheim and slow reinforcements from the pre-positioned equipment POMCUS sites at Kaiserlautern from reaching American forces. A further Army, 6th Combined Arms Army would advance to Heidelberg and form a blocking force to prevent part of VII (US) Corps and II (GE) Corps from advancing north from Southern Germany to counterattack the forces attacking Frankfurt.

In the event these plans were to be far too ambitious given the strictures of both available forces and the time limits imposed by the Stavka, the Soviet High Command. The failings of the plan were to have far reaching consequences for the course of the conflict and its participants.

Nevertheless, at 3am on the morning of July 13th, 1992, massive Russian artillery barrages rained down on NATO positions from the Baltic to the Czech border. Once again Europe was plunged into war.

"Operation Zhukov" I

13th – 16th July 1992

"No plan ever survives contact with the enemy." Helmuth Von Moltke.

Chapter 6

NORTHAG Field Headquarters, somewhere in Western Germany, 04:00 hrs, 13th July 1992.

General Sir Roger Turnbull, British commander of NATO's Northern Army Group, sipped a strong cup of tea, Sergeant Major's tea, so strong that the spoon could stand up by itself in the cup, and studied the first reports of the fighting. He looked up as his second in command, Major General Hardt of the Bundeswehr, entered carrying another bundle of papers.

"What's the latest, Franz?" he asked.

"Confusion," Hardt answered. "The politicians are confused. They thought the peace talks were going well. The Bundeswehr is in an uproar. The Russians are blaming us for the fighting. NATO politicians are also panicking … and some of their senior military, too."

"Christ! We prepared and practised for this for forty-odd years and look at us. All the bloody politicians thought the danger ended when the Wall came down and now their cosy little, lets-all-be-friends, world is falling apart around them." Turnbull shook his head in frustration. "What's the latest situation on the ground?"

Hardt sorted through the papers in his hands and selected one. "We have reports of multiple airborne operations. A helicopter assault, possibly in battalion strength, on Hamburg Airport, another in the vicinity of Bremen, another on Hannover and a possibly larger one on Hameln. The aims of some of these are unclear and we're trying to get more information.

2nd Guards Army appears to be forming two separate thrusts, the northern one towards Hamburg and the southern in the direction of Lüneburg. The Dutch are falling back in front of Hamburg and 3rd Panzer is engaging the southern thrust." He scanned another report. "British 1st Armoured is engaging Soviet forces in possible divisional strength east and southeast of Wolfsburg and 4th Armoured is under pressure north of Bad Harzburg, again possibly by a divisional-sized unit.

Further south the Belgians are engaged in the Harz Mountains but reports from there are few at the moment."

"Casualties?"

"Acceptable so far but it's early days yet."

Turnbull nodded. *That won't last*, he thought as Hardt left him the pile of reports to add to those he already had and returned to the main Operations Room. The NORTHAG commander was left sifting through situation and casualty reports and contemplating what the next few hours would bring.

Southeast of Gross Twülpstedt, FRG, 06:00 hrs 13th July.

"Hello, India One One, this is India One One Alpha. Over."

"India One One. Send. Over."

"India One One Alpha, sighting report. Enemy armour, ten tanks, advancing west, one thousand metres north of my position, 06:00 hours, appear to be Tango Eight Zeros. Will continue to observe. Out."

"India One One. Continue to observe. Out."

33

Corporal Eldon continued to watch the enemy force through the steady drizzle, occasionally wiping moisture from the lenses of his binoculars. More Russian vehicles followed, enough to convince him he was watching a tank battalion. He reported this to his troop leader and prepared to move.

To his left he caught sight of a Lynx helicopter hovering below the treetops preparing to launch an anti-tank missile at the Russian vehicles. As the helicopter rose and a missile sped towards a ZSU 23-4 self-propelled anti-aircraft vehicle he took the opportunity to pull back under cover of the confusion caused by the attack.

"Driver, reverse. Get us out of here, Sandy."

The Scimitar reversed from cover and Sanderson swung it around and headed for their next pre-planned position. Behind them the Lynx also sped westwards, flying nap of the earth, to its next ambush position, leaving the ZSU 23-4 *Shilka* burning in its wake.

An hour later Eldon was peering through the rain watching his opposite number, a BRDM 2 scout car. He tried to ignore the water dripping from the rim of his helmet down the back of his neck. From further east came the sound of artillery fire where the enemy's main body was being pounded by NATO guns.

"Ready when you are, Corp'rl", Trooper Grainger had his eyes glued to the sights for the Scimitar's 30mm cannon.

"Wait." Eldon was making sure the BRDM didn't have any backup. The Soviets were known to reinforce their reconnaissance patrols with Main Battle Tanks. The fact that the Russians appeared to be preparing to move made up his mind for him.

"Right, Grainger. Fire!"

The Scimitar's cannon cracked as a three round burst of armour-piercing rounds punched through the Soviet scout car's thin armour. One of its top hatches burst open but no-one emerged as smoke poured out.

Eldon scanned the area as his vehicle reversed, looking for enemy vehicles. His fears were well-founded as a burst of heavy machine gun fire hammered the position they had just left. Sanderson put some trees between them and the enemy to cover them as they sped off. Eldon was thankful for their good luck, despite his alertness he never saw the vehicle that had fired on them.

By midday Corporal Eldon was the commander of his Troop. This didn't mean much as it only consisted of his vehicle and one other. The Troop had already been a vehicle down with the loss of the Troop Sergeant a week before, lost in the confusion of the German attempts to relieve the trapped forces on the Polish border. His Lieutenant's vehicle had been lost, along with its whole crew, when the Soviets had hammered the edge of the wood where they were concealed with a savage artillery barrage. A direct hit from a 122mm shell had ripped the lightly-armoured Scimitar apart like a tin can.

The name of the game was to cripple the enemy's reconnaissance forces, blinding him while keeping your ability to discover which were his main thrusts. Leaving the enemy to grope around in the dark while you could see his intentions clearly. Unfortunately, in reality it often ended with both sides' reconnaissance forces crippled, leading to a lethal game of blind man's buff as the respective main forces blundered into one another.

At this point the Russian recce was becoming more cautious as the NATO screening forces whittled them down. On the other hand, so was the NATO Covering Force's reconnaissance elements as they also were reduced by casualties. Eldon's troop was currently screening the first of 1st Armoured Division's Battlegroups' delaying positions.

East of Neindorf, FRG, 12:30 pm, 13th July.

The rain had eased off to a drizzle and as a result the mist had lifted and visibility improved. More to the point, cold water had stopped trickling down the back of Eldon's collar, soaking the face veil wrapped around his neck.

From the north and south of his position came the sound of heavy fighting as British Combat Teams were engaged around Almke and west of Rennau. Tank units in battalion strength were attempting to break through either side of Neindorf. Eldon's Troop was waiting for the Soviet tank regiment's second echelon battalion which was expected to assault the important road junction of Neindorf itself.

"Hallo India One One Alpha, this is India One One Charlie. Over."

"India One One Alpha. Go ahead. Over."

"India One One Charlie. Sighting report. Two enemy recce vehicles moving west, five hundred metres east of my position, time now, two Bravo Romeo Delta Mikes. Orders? Out."

"India One One Alpha. Let them pass. Continue to observe. Out."

Eldon switched to the intercom. "Keep your eyes peeled, Grainger, there's Ivan recce on the way. We'll take them out if we can."

A short time later some movement caught his eye to his front. Peering through the dripping foliage he desperately tried to identify what had caused it.

"Grainger, three hundred metres, quarter left, hedgerow, three o'clock, two large trees."

"Got it … vehicle of some kind … could be a BRDM."

"That's one of them. Watch and shoot."

The target vehicle moved along the covered route still partially obscured by the undergrowth. The Scimitar's turret turned slowly, following its progress while Eldon continued to search for any Russian vehicle covering its advance. Thinking itself safe the BRDM accelerated out of cover, sprinting for its next covered position. Anticipating the sudden increase in speed, Grainger led his target and fired a three-round burst, one round smashing into the target's engine compartment.

As the Russian crew scrambled clear of the stricken vehicle, Grainger switched to the co-axial machine gun and began brassing up the area around the BRDM.

"Fuck! Five hundred metres, one o'clock, small building! His fucking wing man! Grainger, rapid fire! Sanderson, reverse!"

The Scimitar shot backwards at speed as 14.7mm rounds from the second BRDM's heavy machine gun tore into the trees around their position. Seconds later the vehicle had put cover between it and the Soviet attacker before moving to its next position. Again the watching and waiting began as the crew recovered after yet another lucky escape.

Within minutes Eldon heard the crack of cannon fire followed by a report from the other Scimitar.

"Hello India One One Alpha, India One One Charlie. Sitrep. One Bravo Romeo Delta Mike destroyed. Out."

"One One Alpha. Roger. Out."

Shortly after India One One Charlie finished off the second BRDM the first Russian tanks appeared.

To the north one of the supporting Battlegroup's Combat Teams, A Company Group, had fallen back from its delaying position around Almke and, to the south, B Company Group had also fallen back after causing delay to the Soviet tank battalion advancing north of the E30 Highway. Now it was the turn of the reserve Combat Team covering the important road junction of the town of Neindorf, facing the Russian tank regiment's second echelon tank battalion. C Company Group's job was to delay the capture of the roads required by the advancing Soviets to maintain the momentum of their advance.

Chapter 7

Northeast of Neindorf, FRG, 13:15 hrs, 13th July.

"Hello Hotel One Zero, this is Hotel One Two Alpha. Over."

"Hotel One Zero. Go ahead. Over."

"Knight, repeat, Knight. Figures approximately three zero, over."

"Hotel One Zero. Roger. Over." Private Robinson, 7 Platoon's radio operator, turned to the platoon commander, Lieutenant Neil. "Cut-off Group, Sir. Enemy tanks in roughly battalion strength."

"Right," Neil looked at the platoon runner. "Tell the Section commanders to stand-to then let Sergeant Duncan know they're coming."

"Hotel One Two Alpha, Hotel One Zero. Understood. Out."

Number One Section's anti-tank gunner, Private Sinclair, looked up from the hastily-dug trench inside the treeline as Hughes, the platoon runner, crashed through the undergrowth and knelt beside Corporal Frame, the Section commander.

"Ivan's coming, Corporal. A battalion of tanks. The Lieutenant says, stand-to."

"Right, lads! Stand-to!"

As his section made ready the word was already spreading to the other section in the ambush's Killing Group, alerted by Frame's shout before Hughes reached them. The Platoon's third section had been split up to form the Cut-off and Stop Groups and one of its fire teams had given warning and was observing the approaching Russian vehicles.

Not far away Sinclair heard the sound of NATO artillery impacting on the advancing Russian battalion. The fire was mainly intended to harass the tanks and force them to speed up to outrun the barrage and close down. With their hatches closed and moving at speed, the vehicles were more vulnerable as they were much less likely to spot any threats. Threats like the hastily-laid minefields that were designed to funnel the tanks into 7 Platoon's ambush, laid where the road passed through a wooded area.

Sinclair nervously checked his Carl Gustav 84mm anti-tank launcher for the umpteenth time. Beside him in the trench Private Jordan settled the butt of his General Purpose Machine Gun more comfortably into his shoulder.

"Dave, does none of this bother ye, pal?" Sinclair felt the need to say something, anything to relieve the tension building up inside him.

"Jordan gave him a cool look. "Nope. Bring it on, mate. We'll slot a few of those cunts then fuck off and do it all again somewhere else."

Sinclair gave a mental shrug and turned back to his weapon. He wondered if Jordan was really as calm as he claimed. Knowing Jordan he suspected that he was actually looking forward to the coming action. Sinclair himself was more apprehensive now that it was just a matter of waiting until the Soviets appeared. He felt himself sweating and quickly took a mouthful of water from his water bottle to try and ease his dry mouth. To try and fight the tension he constantly checked and re-checked his anti-tank weapon. His main fear was that he would freeze when the shooting started and either get himself or someone else killed by failing to act.

150 metres further south of the infantry ambush position a Milan anti-tank missile team were tracking the leading tanks thundering down the road. Out in front of the tanks was a lone BRDM scout car, a survivor of the attrition caused by the NATO reconnaissance units of the Covering Force.

As the BRDM entered the wooded area the Milan team opened fire at the lead tank. At 800 metres the target was well within range and the missile impacted before the tank even knew it was under fire. The HEAT warhead failed to burn through the reactive armour blocks on the glacis plate but the T-80 shuddered to a halt, the impact having stunned the driver.

As the Soviet tank commander shouted frantically at the driver to get them moving again and the following vehicles began to realise they were under attack and fan out, a second missile was on its way. This time the explosion against the vehicle resulted in a jet of molten metal punching through into the tank's interior. The driver survived the hit but was still too stunned to bail out before the vehicle began to burn.

The Milan launched a third missile which missed before the team packed up the launcher and made off deeper into the trees. Behind them the tanks began shelling the treeline as they deployed and closed the range. This continued until they ran into the minefield in front of the wood and lost two tanks, disabled by damaged tracks and running gear.

Meanwhile the BRDM continued along the road as it went through the wood. The British platoon let it pass unmolested as it radioed the following tank companies that the way appeared clear. It halted at the point where the road left the woods and began to curve south towards Neindorf and the junction with the L294 which continued west. Although partially concealed amongst the trees it still presented an easy target for one of the Milan teams concealed in another block of woodland several hundred metres further west. The missile blew the light vehicle apart before its crew realised they were a target.

On the other side of the wood the leading tank company tried to pull back out of the minefield as the following company entered the wood. The company commander was torn between speed and caution. Although the reconnaissance element had reported the wood clear it was perfect for an ambush and there had been no further reports from the scout car.

Caution won, even if only temporarily. The column slowed and the vehicles began to spread out, increasing the distance between each vehicle as the leading tank entered the trees. The tank commanders all had their heads and shoulders out of their hatches, trading safety for the ability to spot any threats, peering nervously at the undergrowth on either side of the road. Behind them the battalion commander continuously exhorted them to keep up the momentum of the advance.

Corporal Evans, Number Two Section commander and leading the Cut-Off Group, realised that they would now be lucky to take out even the leading platoon. Quickly he issued instructions to his section's Carl Gustav gunner beside him in the fighting position.

"Right, Smokey, when Sparky slots the commander of that one," he indicated the third tank from the front. "You light it up."

Private Townley nodded and settled himself into a more comfortable position with the launcher on his shoulder. Beside him Evans opened out the tube of a 66mm disposable, one-shot Light Anti-tank Weapon and placed it on the parapet in front of him. He then tapped Private Sparks on the shoulder and the Light Support Weapon stuttered out a burst.

The Russian tank commander was hurled sideways before collapsing inside the turret. The consternation over the intercom of the tank's gunner as his commander's body slumped down, splashing him with blood, caused the driver to slow down as he tried to find out what was happening. The T-80 shuddered as the driver tried to speed up again and Townley fired. The 84mm round detonated against the side of the hull and the molten jet punched through the armour. Just before the main gun ammunition propellant in the carousel under the turret began to detonate, the driver hurled himself out of his hatch … straight into a burst from Spark's LSW. Seconds later the exploding ammunition dislodged the turret and the vehicle began to burn fiercely, a pillar of fire reaching twenty feet into the air from the open hatches.

The leading T-80 of the following platoon halted as the commander buttoned up and began to reverse, narrowly missing the tank coming up behind it which swerved and also rocked to a halt. Both vehicles began spraying the undergrowth with co-axial machine gun fire, causing the Cut-Off Group to duck down inside their hastily-dug firing position.

At the same time the leading tank of the ambushed platoon had reached Number One Section's position and was hit on the rear sprocket by Sinclair's first shot and its track broken. As the tank rolled to a halt, the broken track unreeling behind it, its commander was hit

41

by small-arms fire as he tried to bring the turret-mounted heavy machine gun into action. Within moments the T-80 was hit by a volley of three LAW rockets and began to burn. None of its crew got out.

Another LAW volley fired by Number Three Section killed the remaining tank of the platoon as Corporal Frame scrambled from his trench.

"Okay, lads. Time to go."

Sinclair and Jordan followed him, Sinclair lumbering along under the weight of the Carl Gustav and Jordan holding the GPMG by its carrying handle as he folded the bipod on the move. Jordan was disappointed that he hadn't got a shot at the tank's crew. In no time they had disappeared into the undergrowth along with the Section's other Fire Team.

Frame's Section was the first to reach the Final RV where the Platoon Sergeant waited with his small group. Lieutenant Neil and the Platoon command group were next followed soon after by the other two sections. A quick check that everyone was present and that there were no enemy troops following them and the Platoon was on its way to the waiting Warrior Infantry Fighting Vehicles.

Frame's Section scrambled on board their Warrior and quickly stored their gear. Sinclair stowed his anti-tank launcher between the back of his seat and the hull and pulled shut the rear door.

"All in! Let's go!" Frame gave the signal to the vehicle commander, Corporal Norman, who gave the order to the driver to move out.

"Hubbard, move out!"

The Platoon's four Warriors burst from the wood and shook out into a wedge formation as they raced westwards across the fields towards the road. 300 metres to their north was another wood that concealed three Milan launchers, 8 Platoon and the Combat Team's attached tank troop, waiting to the rear in hides for the order to move forward and engage the enemy armour. The Platoon headed for a prearranged rendezvous point, skirting the northern edge of Neindorf, where they would wait for the rest of the Combat Team.

Behind the withdrawing British infantry the Soviet tank battalion was attempting to resume the advance. A company of Motor Rifle troops had been brought up, had dismounted and were beginning to clear the wood. As a result the two Milan teams covering the rear of the wood decided it was time to leave. They boarded their Armoured Personnel Carrier and followed 7 Platoon, halting in cover 400 metres away to the south of the rest of the Combat Team's position.

The tank company in the minefield managed to extract themselves at the cost of another disabled vehicle and were regrouping along with the remaining two platoons of the company ambushed in the woods. The battalion's third company moved up and attempted to move round the northern edge of the wood, narrowly missing a smaller minefield north of the road. Behind them NATO artillery began shelling the area where the other companies were regrouping.

The flanking Soviets swung round the northern edge of the trees and headed south between the woods heading for the junction of the L290 and L294 roads. Part way there they ran into another minefield. Within a few minutes three T-80s had been halted by damage to their running gear and other vehicles were halted outside the minefield. As the Russians probed for a way around the obstacle the concealed Milan teams opened fire.

Missiles flew out towards three of the halted tanks and two hit, detonating against the tanks' hulls. Both tanks began to burn before the expanding gases caused by the detonating ammunition propellant tore the turrets off sending them tumbling beside the gutted remains of the hull. The remaining T-80s fired their smoke dischargers for concealment and began shelling the edge of the trees.

The Milan teams were prepared to launch another volley of missiles but one of the Team's Scimitars, watching the wood to the east, reported movement south of the minefield. The Motor Rifle company had finished clearing the wood and the other two tank companies were pushing along the road through the trees after pushing the wreckage of the ambushed T-80s clear of the road to allow passage.

It was time to go. C Company Group had carried out its task which was to delay and cause casualties to the advancing Soviets, not fight them to a standstill. That was the job of the main part of the Division in the Main Defensive Position. The Milan Section and 8 Platoon boarded their vehicles and withdrew to the next position to rejoin 7 Platoon. Only the tank troop remained to provide the final sting in the tail.

Once again NATO supporting artillery began to pound the Russian tanks as they emerged from the wood. This "encouraged" the commanders to batten down their hatches, reducing their vision and the chances of them spotting enemy activity. After a few minutes the barrage changed to smoke shells and, as the pair of Scimitar reconnaissance vehicles took this opportunity to withdraw, the tank troop came into action.

"All Victor Twos, this is Victor Two Zero. Move now! Out".

Lieutenant Jamieson, the commander of A Squadron's 2 Troop, listened to the acknowledgements of his troop's other two tanks as he aided his driver manoeuvre the 62 tonnes of Challenger MBT to the tank scrape the engineers had hastily dug at the wood's edge. To his right and left his Troop Sergeant's and Corporal's tanks also moved forward as they prepared to engage the enemy.

"Ease up a bit, Jenkins. We're coming up to the treeline."

Trooper Jenkins eased the massive vehicles forward and into the tank scrape as Jamieson got his first view of the enemy.

Two T-80s were halted partially in cover at the point where the road emerged from the wood. They were covering a platoon of three tanks who were rolling at speed along the road in the direction of Neindorf. As he watched they changed direction and left the road, heading directly westwards to bypass the built-up area which they saw as another potential ambush site. Behind them more tanks emerged from the trees as the overwatching two tanks moved forward to follow the three thundering over the fields.

Conscious of the fact that there was another tank company on the other side of their wood, Jamieson decided to hit fast and get out.

"Hello, Victor Two One and Victor Two Two, this is Victor Two Zero, over."

"Victor Two One. Roger. Over."

"Victor Two Two. Roger. Over."

"Two rounds each then we pull back. Two One, take the leading tank on the left. Two Two, the leading tank on the right. I'll take the one in the middle. Acknowledge. Two Zero, out."

"Victor Two One. Wilco. Out."

"Victor Two Two. Wilco. Out."

Impatiently Jamieson used his override for the main gun to lay the sight's aiming mark on the target T-80 before relinquishing control of the 120mm gun back to his annoyed gunner.

"Fin! Tank! On!"

The loader had already rammed an armoured-piercing sabot round and bagged charge into the breech before the vehicle had moved forward and now picked up the next round in preparation before responding.

"On!" The gunner had acquired the target and was beginning his engagement sequence, conscious he was firing in anger for the first time.

"Loaded!"

"Fire!"

"Lasing!" The gunner fired the laser range finder, the firing computer made its calculations and automatically aimed off and placed the sight on the target tank. The gunner pressed the trigger. "Firing, now!"

The tank rocked with the recoil of the massive cannon as the 120mm sabot round flew downrange towards its target. Jamieson watched the glowing tracer in the base of the round until it hit the T-80 in a bright flash.

"Target!"

Jamieson waited for the target tank to burn but although it was halted there was no sign of fire.

"Target, go on!"

The engagement sequence was repeated and this time the target began to burn.

"Target, stop!"

Shifting his gaze to the other targets Jamieson was disappointed to see only one other Russian vehicle burning. "Oh for Christ's sake!" *They couldn't hit a barn from the inside*, he thought, irritably and a touch unfairly considering this was their first real action.

"All Victor Two callsigns, this is Victor Two Zero. Withdraw now, out!"

The three Challengers began to reverse out of their tank scrapes as the Russians returned fire. One of the Soviet 125mm rounds caught Two Two a glancing blow which ricocheted off the glacis plate as the tank rocked back on its suspension with the force of the impact. Despite the hail of fire all three vehicles disappeared into the trees without suffering serious damage.

Once fully in cover the tank troop quickly headed westwards following the rest of the combat Team to the rendezvous. To their rear the pair of Scimitars took position to cover them then slipped away to follow them and keep an eye on the following Russians.

Behind them the reduced Soviet tank battalion quickly reorganised and resumed its advance westwards along the L294. Like other leading

Russian units it was being delayed by small actions like this, causing it to deploy which took up valuable time. They were also slowly being bled white, losing destroyed vehicles and also immobilised vehicles which, while able to be repaired, were no longer immediately available to sustain the momentum of the advance.

Chapter 8

NORTHAG Field Headquarters, somewhere in Lower Saxony, FRG, 01:00 hrs, 14th July.

General Turnbull listened wearily to the latest situation report from his staff. He was finding it difficult to concentrate as he had barely managed two hours sleep in the last 24 hours. The news wasn't good but could have been far worse. Major General Hardt was bringing the briefing to a close by briefly summarising the situation in the Northern Army Group area of operations.

"Local Bundeswehr territorial forces are continuing to contain enemy airborne forces in Hamburg, Bremen, Hannover and Hameln. Dutch forces are giving ground northeast of Hamburg as are northern units of German I Corps around Luneburg. There appears to be a developing major thrust in the north of the British sector and they are giving ground in the southern sector. In the south the Belgians are being forced back by a strong Soviet thrust towards Gottingen."

Turnbull massaged his closed eyes with his fingertips then contemplated the large map showing the current dispositions in NORTHAG. Keeping his eyes on the map he said thoughtfully, "It's not really what we expected, is it? They seem much less concentrated … more spread out than their doctrine would normally allow."

He thought about the briefing he had received from the NATO Secretary General's Office a few hours earlier. Soviet sources had made contact with NATO governments through neutral countries in the UN and given an indication of their intentions. NATO was now aware that this was not a full-scale invasion as envisaged during the years of the Warsaw Pact. It was, according to the sources, a limited action with specific objectives, not specified of course, but they would become more obvious as time wore on.

The Soviets had, to a certain extent, uncharacteristically sacrificed their ability to achieve operational surprise to hopefully ensure that the conflict would not escalate out of control due to misunderstanding the Soviet's intentions. The last thing either side wanted was a hasty decision prompted by confusion and panic to use chemical or nuclear weapons. The Soviets had made it clear that they were not contemplating the use of either in a limited conflict.

"You know, I think they're taking tokens … bargaining chips for political negotiations." Turnbull thought he could possibly see a vague pattern emerging. "Hamburg for one … possibly an advance on Bremen to cut off Dutch and Danish forces from the rest of the Army Group. Maybe the push against I British Corps and the Belgians is a diversion?" He turned to his Deputy. "See if you can get more information on what's going on in CENTAG, beyond the reports we've had already. Might confirm the pattern, if there is one."

Hardt hurried away to request the information from Central Army Group HQ leaving Turnbull to try and snatch some sleep before the next briefing due first thing in the morning.

Several hours later and feeling only slightly refreshed by a short sleep, Turnbull finished reading the information received from CENTAG.

In the Central Army Group sector to the south, the Soviet assault was also making progress. Two divisions were pushing along the boundary between III (GE) and V (US) Corps north of Fulda. Another two divisions were pushing through the Fulda Gap itself.

Frankfurt? Wondered Turnbull. *Could be.*

Further south what appeared to be 1st Guards Tank Army was advancing towards Schweinfurt and what appeared to be another force making for Bayreuth. Their purpose was a mystery at the moment.

CENTAG forces were currently withdrawing in good order in front of the advancing Russian forces. In Southern Germany II (GE) Corps was not yet engaged by enemy forces and was preparing to counterattack northwards against the Soviet thrust on Bayreuth. Heavy fighting was taking place at Koblenz and Mannheim between Soviet airborne forces and local German troops and US rear area security forces.

So far things were going well for the Soviets but neither were they going disastrously for NATO. Meanwhile the fighting raged on.

Chapter 9

Southwest of Hattorf, FRG, 04:00 hrs, 14th July.

Corporal Eldon dozed fitfully in his seat while his gunner, Trooper Grainger, peered blearily through the image intensifier watching for the first signs of Russian movement. Above him he could hear rain drumming on the closed hatch and the associated lack of ambient light caused by the cloudy weather was also affecting the night vision device, making his job even harder.

During the night the 2nd echelon of the Soviet tank regiment facing them had reached the line of Highway 39 which ran north-south between Flechtorf and Hattorf before joining the E30 Autobahn 4km further south. They had temporarily halted to reorganise before resuming the advance. As they reorganised, the Division's 2nd echelon, a third tank regiment, was moving forward to continue the push westwards. Its objective was to find or force a crossing of the Mittelland Canal 10 km to the west.

"Corp! Corporal, I've got movement!"

Eldon jerked awake and reached up to open his hatch. Cold rain hit him in the face. "Aww fuck!" Fully awake now he looked down into the turret at Grainger. "What have you got?"

"800 metres, half right, beside the road … in amongst the trees. Possibly some kind of vehicle."

Eldon squinted through the murky pre-dawn half-light, blurred even more by the rain. "What's it look like, now?"

"Still too fuzzy. This fucking rain is fucking the sight picture!"

"Hello India One One Charlie, this is India One One Alpha. We have movement at our two o'clock. See anything? Over." Eldon hoped his other vehicle might provide clearer information.

"India One One Alpha, India One One Charlie. Possible movement south of my position. Will confirm. Out."

They're coming, thought Eldon. *The fuckers are coming. Again.*

The Soviet reconnaissance vehicles were more cautious now than24 hours ago, their casualty rates had taught them that. They crept forward, moving northwards up Highway 39 towards Flechtorf. Behind them raced the lead battalion of the 63rd Guards Tank Regiment, at some point speed and caution were going to collide. "Recce Push", where the cautious advance of reconnaissance forces was overtaken by the main body pushing forward at speed, forcing the reconnaissance units to speed up and invariably degrading their ability to carry out their mission properly, was not unknown to their British counterparts. Unfortunately it frequently proved fatal for the lighter recce forces.

Within a short time the tank battalion commander was urging the reconnaissance screen to move faster as his lead company almost trod on their heels. Inevitably the forced increase in speed, and the resulting decrease in the ability to conceal themselves and observe properly, resulted in casualties amongst the lighter scout cars.

Three rounds from the Warrior's Rarden cannon hammered through the lightly-armoured BRDM. It began to burn, the flames spitting in the drizzle.

"Time to go, Hubbard! Driver, reverse." Corporal Norman turned to face the rear in his hatch to guide Hotel One One back as Private Hubbard quickly reversed from their ambush position. Once the vehicle reached a forestry road running through the woods north of Flechtorf it sped west, joined by No. 2 Section's Warrior from its own ambush.

As the two vehicles moved to rejoin the rest of the platoon they passed a Milan team waiting for the first tanks to appear. Further on a pair of Royal Tank Regiment Challengers also lay in wait, so well concealed that Norman almost failed to spot them. Overhead a light

Gazelle helicopter hovered under the low rain clouds waiting to report the approach of Soviet armour to the anti-tank helicopters readying themselves at the holding rendezvous further to the rear.

As the leading Russian tanks swung west onto the L295 they were unaware that their scouting forces no longer existed, having been knocked out by NATO ambushes. At that point NATO artillery began shelling them, causing them to button up rendering the crews virtually blind. Shellfire blowing away radio aerials made them also deaf in some cases.

Lehre, FRG, 06:00 hrs, 14th July.

The commander of the British 1st Armoured Division had decided that it was time to impose some delay on the Soviet advance. As a result Lt Colonel Masters' Battlegroup was tasked with forming a blocking force at Lehre.

One Milan section was stationed in the woods northwest of the town and the other two in the woods to the east. C Company was split up to provide protection for them. B Company occupied the town itself along with a company of German local Territorial forces. A Squadron's Challengers were concealed in hides in a wood south of the town.

7 Platoon was dug-in some way inside the wood as the edges of woodland were prime targets for artillery hoping to catch any defending infantry or missile teams who had set up there to gain good fields of fire. Positions had been prepared on the treeline but the troops were under cover further in ready to occupy the fighting positions once artillery fire had ceased.

The Soviets 10th Guards Tank Division's original task had been to provide a diversionary attack against 1st Armoured Division while the main assault was against the Belgians to the south. However, the Division's modest success in advancing had earned it some extra support from the commander of 3rd Shock Army. Soviet doctrine was to reinforce success so as a result the 63rd Guards Tank Regiment was now supported by extra artillery and attack helicopters.

The Battlegroup's Reconnaissance detachment gave the first warning of the approaching Soviet armour. Sergeant Mitcham, the Reconnaissance Platoon Sergeant, sent the original sighting report which the Battlegroup HQ passed to its constituent elements. The second indication of their approach was a sudden barrage of shells from an artillery battalion on the northern half of Lehre. This was followed almost immediately by similar-sized artillery strikes on the woods held by C Company.

Neil's Platoon huddled in their trenches as high explosives hammered the trees a hundred metres to their front. The troops sheltered in the shelter bays at each end of their four-man trench as the ground shuddered under the impacts. The air was filled with flying clods of earth, wood splinters and shrapnel. Smoke and the stench of high-explosives hung in the air.

Sinclair and Jordan huddled together, flinching every time the ground heaved. Both men were aware that the Platoon's positions were well inside the safe distance foe field artillery and wished the positions had been dug further into the woods despite the extra time it would have taken to occupy their battle positions when the barrage ceased.

At the other end of the trench Corporal Frame hunched up alone. As the earth bucked and heaved he worried less about himself and more about how his Section was faring. In Fire Team Delta's trench Lance Corporal Davis looked on in disgust as Private Lister tried to squeeze himself further into the corner of the trench. Lister held his Light Support Weapon tightly to his chest with both hands. He was sobbing and his eyes were screwed tightly shut. Davis didn't realise that he himself involuntarily jumped slightly every time a shell landed.

Although to those on the receiving end the barrage seemed to last for hours it only lasted for a few minutes. The sudden silence when it ceased left the troops deafened and stunned.

"Stand to! Stand to!" Sergeant Duncan's voice rang through the air and cut through their daze.

Frame scrambled from the shelter bay and hauled himself out of the trench. He paused as Sinclair and Jordan followed him and looked around for the rest of his Section. Through the lingering smoke he saw Davis leading the other Fire Team and felt relief that his Section appeared to be unscathed. Coughing from the smoke and fumes he followed them towards the battle positions as they clambered over fallen trees and forced their way through broken branches and larger tree limbs strewn over the forest floor.

Sinclair was panting under the weight of his Carl Gustav launcher by the time he lowered himself into his firing position. He placed his assault rifle on the front parapet beside the anti-tank weapon. Jordan was already readying his machine gun. He slammed shut the top cover on the newly-loaded 200 round belt and cocked the weapon while scanning for the first sight of the enemy. Sinclair loaded a round into his launcher and stared through the foliage in front of the trench.

Frame looked over towards his other Fire Team's trench and saw Private Waters, the Reservist who had only joined the Section in the run up to the start of hostilities, jump back under cover after clearing a fallen tree limb that had been blocking their arc of fire. Somewhere to the north the Battlegroup's mortar platoon was laying down smoke on the advancing enemy.

The Russian lead tank company spread out into an attack formation as it came in sight of Lehre. Some instinct warned the company commander that the town was defended. This was confirmed a few moments later as three Milan missiles, fired by the German Home-Defence troops, flew towards the advancing armour.

In reply the Soviet tanks opened fire with their co-axial machine guns, spraying the edge of the town with rounds. The tactic unnerved the inexperienced missile teams and two of the missiles missed their targets. The third hit and a T-80 rolled to a halt, spewing smoke as its crew bailed out. German machine gun fire reached out towards the crew, catching the driver before he could reach cover.

The remaining tanks sped on until they ran into a hurriedly-laid minefield on either side of the road running into the town. Two tanks, one either side of the road, detonated mines and halted, their running gear heavily damaged. Machine gun fire and anti-personnel mines sown amongst the heavier anti-tank mines took their toll of the damaged tanks' escaping crews.

More Milan missiles reached out to the two damaged tanks. Soon they were both burning, wracked by internal explosions as their ammunition detonated. The rest of the tank company fired their smoke dischargers and withdrew out of range, taking cover in a village to the northeast.

The men of 7 Platoon watched the action under orders not to open fire. The Milan teams lining the treeline remained in cover, waiting to surprise the inevitable attempt to outflank the town on either side. Again, the gap between the built-up area and the woods was blocked at the south side of Lehre by hastily-laid minefields.

For the first time in 24 hours the Soviet advance had been halted, even if only temporarily, in BAOR's sector. The 10th Guards Tank Division's lead elements began to regroup and take stock. The halt allowed them to bring up badly-needed supplies and hurriedly carry out essential vehicle maintenance as they prepared for a deliberate attack to punch through the blocking position. The pause, however, would be brief.

Chapter 10

Lehre, FRG, 07:30 hrs, 14th July.

A brief but intense artillery barrage on the northern part of the town heralded the resumption of the Soviet advance. Despite defensive positions prepared by the Battlegroup's engineer platoon and reinforced cellars in the houses, casualties mounted, particularly amongst the German defenders.

The high explosive was followed by a smoke barrage which blanketed the area held by the German missile teams and outposts and B Company's 4 Platoon. At the same time the Soviet tank battalion began to move forward out of their concealment in the village. One company veered left to bypass Lehre to the east while a second went right flanking to the west. The original, reduced, company followed in reserve along with a Motor Rifle company from the divisional reserve.

The battalion commander had no intention of becoming bogged down in fighting within the town itself. His instructions were to press on and keep the advance moving. He fully intended to bypass any pockets of resistance and leave them to be mopped up by follow-on forces. Unfortunately for him, the NATO forces had other ideas.

The battalion's 3rd Company crossed the small stream that ran across its front without much difficulty and began to advance past the east side of Lehre as artillery fire, both high explosives and smoke, began to pound the eastern half of the town. As the tanks thundered past, several missiles flew from the town. They all missed as their operators were suppressed or killed by the artillery fire.

However, the ineffective missile attacks did distract the tank crews' attention from the real source of danger, the Milan section in the woods on their left flank. Five missiles sped towards the unsuspecting tank company. With no distractions to disturb their aim the operators were able to concentrate on their targets. Despite the fact that the vehicles were moving at speed, four of the five struck their targets. All four T-80s rolled to a stop, trailing smoke and shedding external stowage. Surviving crew members began to bail out as the tanks burst into flames.

The remaining half dozen tanks increased speed to escape the killing ground, spewing white smoke from their smoke generators to create a concealing screen. Unfortunately the Milan launchers were equipped with MIRA thermal imaging sights which could penetrate the smoke. Within minutes another two tanks had been hit. The end came for the company as the remaining four tanks raced into the minefield laid between the southern edge of the wood and the edge of Lehre. All four T-80s suffered mobility kills as their damaged running gear brought them to a halt.

As the 3rd Company was destroyed the supporting reduced 2nd Company and its accompanying Motor Rifle company came under ATGW attack from the Milan section positioned between 7 and 9 Platoons in the northern part of the wood. All five missiles hit and three tanks were put out of action. The remaining two were saved from serious damage by their reactive armour bricks despite the crews suffering from shock caused by the missiles' impact.

Both company commanders reacted aggressively, turning towards the trees and firing at the area where the missile fire appeared to come from as they raced into the attack. 125mm tank guns and 30mm BMP cannon hammered the treeline and the Milan section. Although firing on the move made it difficult to actually hit any targets, the sheer weight of fire suppressed the Milan teams and prevented more missiles being fired.

After suffering several casualties the Milan teams began to withdraw back to their transport hidden deeper in the trees. A final missile fired by the northernmost pair of launchers, off on a flank, gutted a BMP, killing its crew and passengers. Then the Milan section was gone. The withdrawing anti-tank teams rendezvousing with their FV432s concealed along a narrow lane running through the woods. Behind them the Motor Rifle troops were dismounting and assaulting their abandoned positions.

This brought the Russian infantry within the range of 7 Platoon. Using disposable Light Anti-tank Weapons the concealed infantry engaged the BMPs as they disgorged their troops. Three BMPs were hit and began to burn, many of their passengers dead or wounded around them.

Sinclair took aim with his Carl Gustav MAW as Jordan finished loading a projectile and slapped him on the shoulder. He felt his whole body shaken as the 84mm round flew towards a BMP and detonated on its sloping glacis plate. The vehicle shuddered and began to lurch backwards until it was hit by two 66mm LAW rounds which set it ablaze.

Jordan's GPMG was hammering rounds at the Russian infantry attempting to storm the trench line as Sinclair picked up his rifle to defend the trench. Frame was busy directing his Section's fire as the Soviet infantry fought their way closer. A fierce firefight raged as the Motor Riflemen sought to gain a foothold at the edge of the trees to enable them to storm the trenches. Small arms fire crackled and a storm of rounds poured from both sides, accompanied by heavier cannon fire from the surviving BMPs trying to suppress or destroy the British defenders.

The assault was finally repulsed by the Platoon's Warriors, brought forward from their hides, driving almost up to the trenches and using their machine guns and cannon to pound the remains of the Motor Rifle company. The surviving Russian infantry fell back and reboarded the remaining BMPs, the lucky few cramming into the passenger compartments and the rest scrambling to find handholds on the outside of the hull. Covered by fire from the remaining tanks they withdrew under cover of smoke from their smoke dischargers as machine gun fire swept men from their hulls.

As the battered Soviets pulled back to take cover in the village they had previously occupied, Corporal Frame scrambled out of the trench.

"Right, lads! Time to go!"

He reached down and Sinclair handed the Carl Gustav up to him as he hauled himself out of the trench. Frame paused for a second to check on the rest of his Section. Nearby he saw Lance Corporal Davis chivvying Private Lister deeper into the wood behind Clark and Waters. Behind them the Platoon's Warriors reversed from their positions and withdrew deeper into cover.

Sergeant Duncan waited further back checking that all the Platoon were present and that no Russian stragglers were following them. Once everyone was accounted for he followed the last of the Milan teams, struggling under the load of launcher and missiles, back to the shelter of the trenches deeper inside the trees.

"For what we are about to receive … " he muttered as he scrambled down into his trench.

Within minutes a deluge of shells began to pound the edge of the woods where the British had been. Wrecked BMPs were beaten into scrap metal and several wounded Motor Riflemen, left behind in the mad scramble to fall back, were killed. Huddled in their trenches the men of 7 Platoon were stunned but suffered no further casualties.

On the far side of Lehre the Soviet 1St Company had also run into another Milan section firing from the woods to the northwest. Already three tanks were burning as the remainder raced south making smoke only to run into yet another hastily-laid minefield. As the surviving mobile tanks milled about in their smokescreen, still attempting to find a path past the minefield, the Battlegroup's tank squadron was brought into action. A troop of Challengers was ordered from their hides to engage the survivors.

The Squadron's 3 Troop Sergeant, Sergeant Turner, guided his driver into the tank scrape the engineers had dug on the edge of the trees.

"Take it forward a tad. That's it. Driver, prepare to halt." The 60 tonne vehicle slowly rolled forward into the position. "Driver, halt."

Turner dropped into the turret and put his face to the tank commander's sight.

"Target front!" he ordered, laying the 120mm gun on one of the T-80s, clearly visible through the Thermal Imaging sight, moving through the smoke.

"Fin, tank, on!" Turner passed control of the gun to his gunner.

Below him, in the gunner's position, Trooper Cox acquired the target vehicle in his own sights. "On!"

On the other side of the massive gun breech, Brinkworth, the loader, had thrust an APFSDS or "Fin" round into the breech followed by a bagged charge, closed the breech and checked the turret safety switch was on live. Once done he shouted, "loaded!" to let the gunner and commander know the gun was ready.

Cox concentrated on his target as Turner gave the order, "fire!" As he fired the laser rangefinder he saw the oval ballistic aiming mark appear in the sight picture around the target tank. It almost immediately shifted from its position onto the engraved graticule pattern of lines in the sight as the computer calculated the correct elevation and aim off for the gun. A second later the gun automatically drove up and the ellipse once again surrounded the target.

"Firing now!" shouted Cox as he pressed the trigger on his joystick which fired the gun. The massive vehicle rocked slightly as the 120mm gun hurled the projectile at the target with a loud explosion and a bright flash. As the gun returned to battery after recoiling into the cramped confines of the turret a spurt of smoke gushed from the muzzle.

Turner watched the tracer in the base of the tungsten dart fly towards the target tank after the sabot split away. There was a bright flash as it struck the T-80 followed by a massive explosion as it detonated the ammunition in the Russian tank's autoloader carousel under the turret floor. The T-80's turret was hurled into the air by the pressure of the expanding gases, landing next to the blazing hull.

"Target!" Even Turner was shocked at the sight. This was the first time he had watched a tank die and was appalled at how easily and quickly such a heavily-armoured vehicle could be destroyed.

"Target stop!"

Turner scanned the front again. There were more tanks burning in the smoke, glowing white in the TOGS Thermal Imaging sight. There were also still targets, targets which fired back.

"Target front!"

The Soviet divisional commander had now decided to find an alternative route, one that was less well-defended. The remains of the tank battalion outside Lehre were left in place to screen, or at least provide warning if the British Battlegroup moved north, the advance of 10th Guards Tank Division. The main force turned northwards through Gross Brunsrode before resuming the westward march towards Essenrode.

East of Lehre, FRG, 10:00 hrs, 14th July.

Lieutenant Neil's Platoon were busy reorganising in their woodland hide. Some of the Platoon were manning observation posts while others were policing up the battlefield and dealing with casualties. The Company Quartermaster Sergeant had brought up supplies and replacements from the supply echelon and these were being distributed.

Hubbard was checking the tracks on the Warrior and was currently examining the damage to the vehicle's side add-on armour panels caused by a glancing hit from a 30mm cannon shell. He was only now realising how close they had come to disaster. He suppressed a shudder as he remembered the way the vehicle had rocked under the impact of the shell.

"Where's the brew, Clarkie?" he shouted.

"Fuck's sake, Smiler! Have some patience."

Private Clark was inside the vehicle operating the built-in Boiling Vessel. He climbed out of the rear door with the water bottle cups of tea. He handed one to Hubbard.

"Too kind," Sergeant Duncan had appeared from nowhere and plucked the other cup from Clark's hand before he could raise it to his lips. "Oh, yes. NATO standard, just the way I like it. You've trained him well, Smiler."

"Like one of the PG Chimps, Sergeant. In looks as well as skills," Hubbard smiled, his teeth appearing very white against his dark skin, sipping his brew.

"Fuck off, Smiler." Clark sulked back into the Warrior to get another tea.

Duncan nodded towards Privates Townley and Sparks who were approaching laden with supplies. "Get the ammo and rations sorted out, we'll be moving soon. Where's Frame?"

Hubbard hooked a thumb towards the edge of the wood. "He's up there with the rest of the Section."

"Right." Duncan flung the dregs of his drink into the undergrowth and handed the empty cup to Hubbard. "Get everything sorted out and stowed away as quick as you can." He turned and headed for the fighting positions as Clark again appeared from the passenger compartment.

Townley and Sparks dumped an ammunition box beside the tracks. "There you go, Smiler. More ammo for you. Enjoy." Before turning back to fetch more supplies.

Hubbard pointed at the box. "There you go, Clarkie. Start filling magazines."

"Fuck off, Smiler. Lemme drink me brew first."

"Get it done, Clark. You can drink tea and fill mags at the same time." Corporal Norman had poked his head from the turret hatch briefly then disappeared back into the turret muttering to himself. "Gobby prick."

Taylor looked at him from the gunner's seat. "Clarkie being a dick again?" Norman nodded. Clark was not the most popular member of the Section.

A few minutes later Corporal Frame and the rest of the Section returned.

"Get a brew on, Clarkie." Frame slumped down and propped his back up against one of the Warrior's wheels as Clark stamped back into the vehicle. The others sat around and began to field strip and clean their weapons.

"Bad?" Hubbard asked Sinclair.

Sinclair looked up and nodded before carefully dropping his rifle's gas plug into his helmet. Hubbard looked around at the others, all quiet, all grubby, there was no conversation or banter. Even Clark had the sense to be quiet as he collected their water bottle cups.

Within the hour the Battlegroup was again on the move, moving westwards back into reserve with the rest of the Brigade. To their north the sound of battle marked where 10th Guards Tank Division continued their push towards the Mittelland Canal.

Chapter 11

The 10th Guards Tank Division's original mission had been to mount diversionary attacks against the British 1st Armoured Division to prevent it intervening against the main thrust further south. The Soviet division, although having suffered heavy casualties, was making better progress than had been expected. As a result, following the Soviet doctrine of reinforcing success, the commander of 3rd Shock Army allocated further resources, extra artillery and attack helicopters, to the division. It would shortly prove that the commander's confidence in it was justified.

Northeast of Meinholz, FRG, 08:00 hrs, 15th July.

The German Territorial platoon guarding the small road bridge over the Mittelland Canal had been listening to the sound of fighting coming ever closer for the past several hours. Like all the other bridges over the canal it had been prepared for demolition. Most had already been blown, only a few minor crossings like this one were left up temporarily until the last of the Covering Force were across the canal.

The crew of the BRDM scout car who were observing them from the woods outside Abbesbüttel also knew that it was one of the few bridges still up. They had been lucky and managed to slip through a gap in the NATO reconnaissance screen. The fact that the bridge was still in one piece had been reported back to Division and heavy forces were on their way to attempt to seize the crossing.

Within the hour the first of the withdrawing NATO units reached the bridge. Supply units were the first to cross, the watching reconnaissance unit observed the trucks of an Immediate Replenishment Group with itchy trigger fingers. Soon they were followed by damaged vehicles and those carrying the wounded. After the final vehicles, a Chieftain Armoured Recovery Vehicle towing a

Challenger with heavy turret damage, there was a pause as the sound of fighting drew closer.

As it became clear to the bridge defenders that the withdrawing British forces had failed to "break clean" there was an increase in their activity, hurriedly improving their defensive positions. This was interrupted by a sudden mortar barrage which landed on or around the bridge. The defenders quickly took cover, dragging their wounded with them.

A group of three Warriors appeared from the town, speeding towards the bridge with their turrets reversed covering their rear. They raced over the bridge and took cover in the undergrowth lining the canal beyond. Another pair broke from the cover of the built-up area and headed for the bridge.

One of them failed to make it. An anti-tank missile, fired from an Mi-24 Hind attack helicopter hovering to the north, smashed into the leading vehicle. The Warrior slewed to a halt spewing smoke as the rear door was blown open. Wounded men sprawled out as the vehicle began to burn.

One of the Territorials fired a Stinger hand-held anti-aircraft missile at the Hind which pumped out decoy flares causing the missile to miss. In return the Hind strafed the area around the bridge with heavy machine gun fire from its rotary 12.7mm four-barrelled gun. One of the first casualties was the exposed Stinger operator.

There was the crash of tank cannon in the town and two Challengers ran along the road at high speed, turrets to the rear seeking targets. They reached the trees lining the canal bank unscathed due to the Hind having used up all its anti-tank missiles and took up positions to cover the exit from the town.

A third Challenger appeared and headed for the bridge but only made it halfway before being hit by several rounds from tank cannon. The British tank burst into flames and spewed smoke as several T-80s appeared from the built-up area. The two covering Challengers opened fire and a short, sharp close range firefight took place which resulted in one Challenger and ywo T-80s being knocked out.

The surviving T-80s were joined by another three and half a dozen BMPs. The senior Russian officer, a *Leytenant* commanding the survivors of a Motor Rifle company, saw an opportunity to seize a crossing over the Mittelland Canal. He ordered the Russian force to rush the bridge.

Firing its smoke dischargers the surviving Challenger pulled out of its position and raced across the bridge. The surviving German infantry on the east bank also abandoned their trenches and scrambled after the British tank across the bridge. The advancing Soviets chivvied them on with heavy but inaccurate machine gun fire. The Hind joined in, spraying the bridge with heavy machine gun fire.

As the Challenger cleared the bridge the covering Warriors opened up with their 30mm cannon, targeting the lead T-80 which was thundering across the bridge followed by a pair of BMPs. Cannon shells careened off the bridge and smashed external stowage on the Russian vehicles as well as killing or wounding some German stragglers. A LAW round caught the tank a glancing blow, defeated by the reactive armour bricks.

As the first enemy vehicles left the bridge chaos ensued amongst the surviving defenders. Russian infantry dismounted and swung straight into the assault on the trenches on the west bank of the canal. Fire from the Warriors brewed up both BMPs but several more tanks and BMPs rushed across the crossing. In the confused melee around the bridge approaches the demolition engineers became casualties before they could blow the bridge.

Seeing that the bridge had been taken, the remains of the British Combat Team took advantage of the confusion to withdraw, including the Challenger which managed to escape while the Soviet tanks were more concerned with infantry with LAWs. Behind them the Soviets began to consolidate their unexpected gain. They now had a bridgehead over the Mittelland Canal and what had been a diversionary action had now developed into a major thrust against NATO.

The reports of the capture of the bridge at Meinholz caused concern at 1St Armoured Division HQ. The nearest available force for a counterattack was the British Battlegroup which had just crossed the canal at various points. The battered and understrength force needed time to reorganise and resupply before it would be able to counterattack the bridgehead. The immediate response was to task the RAF with preventing, or at least slowing, the Soviet build up.

In the meantime the Soviets raced to bring up reinforcements and push them across the canal. By the time the first air raid took place, a battered tank battalion and an understrength Motor Rifle battalion had crossed into the bridgehead. A hasty defence was soon organised, awaiting the inevitable attempt by NATO to push them back across the canal.

A pair of Tornados flew at low-level following the canal from the southwest. At this point the Soviets had been unable to bring forward much in the way of air defence although a single ZSU 23-4 Shilka had been found to back up the hand-held SAM launchers belonging to the Motor Rifle troops.

The Tornados attacked into a blizzard of SA 7 Grail missiles and a quadruple stream of 23mm rounds. One of the RAF aircraft was lost but the other damaged the bridge with a near miss. The bridge was still standing but unuseable, even if only temporarily. For the immediate future the Soviets would be unable to reinforce the bridgehead.

The Russians hurriedly moved forward engineers and anti-aircraft assets and pushed as many units as they could towards the bridgehead, including those which had suffered heavy casualties and were rebuilding. It was a race to repair the bridge and reinforce the bridgehead before NATO could destroy the bridge and counterattack the forces already across the canal. Infantry and man-portable anti-tank weapons could still use the bridge but not heavy vehicles.

For most of the day NATO mounted a series of air strikes against the crossing point but the growing strength of the air defences and mounting casualties amongst the attacking aircraft caused further strikes to be called off. No further damage was caused to the bridge despite the loss of several RAF and Luftwaffe aircraft.

It took until late afternoon for the British Battlegroup to reorganise and resupply despite the insistence of Division and Corps HQ that the bridgehead was to be assaulted as soon as possible. Air attacks on supply units and the Battlegroup itself as it moved forward contributed significantly to the delay.

The Soviet bridgehead over the Mittelland Canal, near Meinholz, FRG, 16:45 hrs, 15th July.

The Royal Tank Regiment Battlegroup's assault on the bridgehead commenced with a short, sharp bombardment of the hamlet of Meinholz itself. This was followed by smoke shells to cover the assault. While this was going on the Fire Support Group, consisting of a troop of tanks, took up position to cover the advancing troops. At the same time an infantry platoon moved out to clear the wood to the north.

Using their Thermal Imagers the Fire Support tanks identified several concealed tanks amongst the buildings and began to engage them. Two T-80s were hit and others were forced further into cover. Their return fire was ineffective. Small-arms fire came from the wood as the infantry platoon ran into Russian Motor Riflemen in the trees. Simultaneously the artillery again began to bombard the small cluster of buildings as the main assault began.

Two tank troops moved out first, one on either side of the village to provide suppressive fire. Behind them an infantry platoon, a composite unit put together from two understrength platoons, raced towards the nearest building accompanied by two Challengers who would provide intimate support for the infantry. The fire support tanks continued to fire on any targets which appeared in the village. Deeper in the bridgehead two RAF Harriers carried out an airstrike on the bridge itself while the defenders were distracted. Both were

69

damaged by anti-aircraft fire before releasing their ordnance and limped off westwards.

The left flank Assault Troop was hit by tank fire from the wood to the north. The T-80s concealed in the treeline were still being protected from the British infantry platoon tasked with clearing the wood by their accompanying infantry escort. Two of the Challengers were hit and the third withdrew under cover of smoke while returning fire, destroying one of the ambushing tanks. The other two Challengers were abandoned, losing several of their crewmen in the process.

On the other flank the other Assault Troop was suppressing the Russians amongst the buildings, losing one tank to an anti-tank missile. They managed to pick off a T-80 which unwittingly exposed itself through the smoke. They also took a toll of camouflaged missile teams.

The assaulting infantry platoon managed to reach the edge of the village without any casualties, shot on to the objective by the Intimate Support tanks. They dismounted amongst some small trees as their Warriors hammered any likely concealment with their cannon and co-axial machine guns. Immediately both vehicles and dismounts were lashed by small-arms and RPG fire through the smoke from infantry concealed in the rubble of a nearby building. The fighting in the village quickly bogged down in a fierce firefight.

Further east the Soviet engineers were labouring hard to make the canal bridge strong enough for armour to cross. British artillery harassing fire was causing a steady drain of casualties. Air raids also caused casualties to reinforcements moving forward or concealed nearby in and around Abbesbüttel waiting for the bridge to be repaired. NATO losses in ground-attack aircraft were also substantial.

Eventually the infantry platoon clearing the woods to the north managed to force the Soviet infantry in the woods to withdraw enough to enable them to get amongst the tanks and engage them with LAWs. A confused action began amongst the trees as infantry hunted T-80s which were almost blind at such close quarters. The surviving Russian infantry in turn hunted the anti-tank teams and tried to protect the heavy armour.

After a short time the few remaining Motor Riflemen were hunted down or dispersed and the two remaining T-80s crashed out into the open where they could defend themselves better. Immediately they were engaged by the surviving Challenger of the Assault Troop which had withdrawn earlier. Both T-80s were knocked out before they could return fire effectively.

The British infantry quickly reorganised, checking their casualties and redistributing ammunition. The latter proved to be low and there was a short pause as more ammunition and LAWs were brought up and the wounded and a few prisoners evacuated. As soon as this was completed the diminished platoon remounted their IFVs and were driving south to join the struggle for the village. On the way they raced past members of the attached REME Light Aid Detachment working to repair or recover the two Challengers knocked out earlier.

These reinforcements turned the tide in the village and within a relatively short space of time the battered remains of the two British platoons controlled most of the scattered piles of smoking rubble that was all that was left of Meinholz. Even as the infantry policed up the area and began the process of winkling out any Russian survivors who still showed signs of a fight, the Battlegroup commander ordered the tank squadron that had been held in reserve to move forward past Meinholz and assault the bridge itself.

Two troops swung round to the north of the village while the other two troops swung south along the canal bank. As they passed the three Challengers of the surviving Assault Troop, hull down east of the village protecting the consolidating infantry from any counterattack, Russian artillery began to fall on the rubble.

Mortars, firing from beyond the canal, laid a smokescreen on the approaches to the bridge as the Challengers manoeuvred forward. The tanks switched to thermal imaging as the first anti-tank missiles reached out towards them. The tanks fired back with both main guns and co-axial machine guns to try and put the missile operators off their aim or destroy the launchers.

Two tanks of one troop were advancing when the third tank, in an overwatch position, picked up a Soviet tank manoeuvring in the smoke. It fired and hit the T-80 with its second shot. Behind it more tanks could be seen taking up better fire positions. The British tanks continued to advance, firing from the short halt as Soviet tanks became visible in their thermal imaging sights. The enemy tanks returned fire and anti-tank missiles began to score hits. Three of the Challengers were damaged, two began to withdraw and the third was abandoned by its crew. It was hit several more times and began to burn.

Despite several Russian tanks being knocked out the amount of fire coming at the British tanks increased rather than decreased. Another two Challengers were hit and damaged before the Squadron commander realised that the number of Russian tanks were increasing. It soon became clear that the enemy were being reinforced and that had to mean that the bridge had been repaired enough to take heavy armoured vehicles.

As the pressure increased the British armour began to fall back. In Meinholz the infantry took up defensive positions and anti-tank missile teams were brought forward, some to the village and some to positions lining the woods to the north. The covering Assault Troop was joined by the three tanks of the Fire Support Group and a pair of Strikers with their long-range Swingfire ATGWs found concealment in the rubble of the hamlet. The other tank squadron pulled back beyond the village to be used as a reserve for counterattacking any breakthroughs.

The Battlegroup's Forward Observation Officer called down more artillery on the bridge and the REME Light Aid Detachment worked frantically to repair what damaged tanks it could, evacuating those beyond their resources to the rear. The counterattack had failed and was now turning into a holding action to prevent the Soviets from breaking out of the bridgehead.

Chapter 12

Meinholz, FRG, 01:00 hrs, 16th July.

Flames from a burning Challenger illuminated a passing T-80, ammunition inside the blazing vehicle crackled as it cooked off. More vehicles of both sides burned on the open ground between the blazing rubble of Meinholz and the wood to the north. Dotting the darkness between there and the bridge were the fires of more burning armoured vehicles. Behind the T-80 more Soviet armour moved westwards, pressing the remains of the retreating British Battlegroup.

10th Guards Tank Division had thrown everything they had into the bridgehead, aided by a second bridge thrown up by their engineers. The Royal Tank Regiment Battlegroup had held two assaults but, despite priority on artillery support and some anti-tank helicopter reinforcements, were broken by the third. The Brigade commander, acutely aware that the Soviet breakthrough had to be prevented but that this force made up a third of 1st Armoured Division's reserve brigade, had made the decision to pull back what was left rather than see it destroyed and badly weaken the Divisional reserve.

Now the battered tank regiments of the Soviet division were flooding westwards, trying to build up enough momentum to propel them deep into the NATO rear area. Fortunately for NATO, and unfortunately for the commander of 3rd Shock Army, all four of the Army's divisions were already committed so there were none spare to use as an Operational Manoeuvre Group which could be hurled far into NOTHAG's rear area, dislocating the whole British Corps' defence. The flaw of using a plan originally designed for much larger forces than were currently available was now becoming obvious.

NORTHAG Field HQ, somewhere west of Hannover, FRG, 03:15 hrs, 16th July.

The staff of NORTHAG were working in a state of controlled chaos, fighting fatigue as well as the Russians after four days of high-intensity war. The breakthrough north of the Mittelland Canal had taken I British Corps by surprise and was threatening its left flank which should have been protected by the canal. That same waterway was now protecting the Soviet 10th Guards Tank Division's flank as it used the E30 Autobahn to advance rapidly towards Hannover.

The result of this rapid advance was that 1st Armoured Division's 12 Armoured Brigade's main line of defence along the Salzgitter Branch Canal was in danger of being outflanked. If the Brigade was destroyed it would create a hole in I (BR) Corps' defence which could result in the loss of all the territory between Braunschweig and the River Leine.

General Turnbull was studying the map of the area east of Hannover as it was constantly updated by his staff.

"What's the latest in the British sector, Franz?" he asked as Major General Hardt approached.

"22 Armoured Brigade is pulling back west of Peine and preparing to dig-in between Burgdorf and Sehnde. A Battlegroup of 7 Armoured Brigade is trying to slow them down but it's been badly damaged and isn't slowing them much. The rest of the Brigade is now concentrating south of the canal between Salzgitter and Ilsede ready to counterattack. 12 Armoured Brigade is still in position along the branch canal.

"What's happening further south with 4th Armoured?"

"They're still falling back under pressure from 12th Guards Tank Division. 11 Armoured Brigade mounted some counterattacks from the north which slowed Ivan down but the Division is pulling back to a line along the E4 southeast of Hildesheim." Hardt glanced at another report in his hand. "3rd Shock Army's main thrust is still against the Belgians. They're being pushed hard by two Tank Divisions, 47th

74

Guards and 7th Guards, and are falling back rapidly. The Russian objective, in the short term, appears to be Gottingen."

Without taking his eyes off the map, Turnbull began to rap out orders, acting as much in his dual role a commander of BAOR as commander of NORTHAG. "22 Brigade will form a blocking position, but not as far west as the Burgdorf-Lehre-Sehnde line. Somewhere between that line and Peine will do. Pull back the Royal Tank Regiment Battlegroup south of the canal. They're spent, rest them and reconstitute as best you can. The rest of 7 Brigade to prepare to counterattack northwards, across the canal, against 10th Guards Tank Division. I want them moving as soon as possible."

He paused for a second, looking further north into the area of responsibility of I (GE) Corps. "See if I German Corps can do anything from the north. Even if they can slow Ivan down it'll give us time to create a blocking position." He turned to Hardt, "Get the orders off to I British Corps and I German Corps straight away."

As Hardt turned away to issue the orders he heard Turnbull muttering to himself.

"Time … time. It's all about time … "

South of Ilsede, FRG, 04:00 hrs, 16th July.

Lt-Colonel Masters' Battlegroup had recrossed the Mittelland Canal late on the afternoon of 15th July and eventually moved into woods east of Ilsede to rest and resupply. The stowing of gear and ammunition and the routine maintenance of vehicles had barely finished and the exhausted troops were now trying to get some sleep. Even now the weary men of the REME Light Aid Detachment were still working on damaged vehicles trying to get as many fighting vehicles as possible up and running.

Sergeant Duncan was asleep on a groundsheet beneath a tarpaulin stretched from the deck of his Warrior to the ground, forming an open-ended tent. The rest of the Platoon HQ Section was lined up in sleeping bags alongside him. He was woken by a hand urgently shaking his shoulder.

"Sergeant! Sergeant!"

Duncan came awake with an annoyed grunt and squinted up at the dark form kneeling beside him.

"The Lieutenant wants you, Sergeant." The voice was that of Private Sparks, currently on sentry duty. "He's over here." He stood up and pointed off into the darkness.

Duncan wearily pulled himself out of his sleeping bad and groped for his webbing, helmet and rifle. "Come on then." Sparks led the way to where Lieutenant Neil stood beside No. 1 Section's Warrior, almost invisible against its black bulk.

"Sir."

"I've just been to a company "O" group, Sergeant. There's been a warning order from Brigade. "O" groups for section commanders in fifteen minutes at my wagon."

"Sir." Duncan turned and made his way to wake the three section commanders and prepare the Platoon for upcoming action.

Fifteen minutes later Neil and Duncan were huddled under a tarpaulin rigged up on the opposite side of the vehicle from the sleeping HQ Section with Corporals Frame, Evans and Hastie. Further cover had been suspended over the open ends to try and make light-proof. Neil had used "black nasty" tape to fasten a map to the slab of composite armour mounted on the side of the Warrior's hull.

"Right, listen in. We've received a warning order for a counterattack against a breakthrough by Ivan north of the Mittelland Canal.

Firstly. Ground. Due to the enemy moving fast we only have a general area for the operation. We can expect to encounter the enemy west of Peine but this is unconfirmed at this time."

76

There was a slight stir amongst the NCOs at the vague nature of the briefing as they scanned their maps in the area around Peine.

"Situation. Enemy forces. 10th Guards Tank Division bounced the canal and formed a bridge head at Meinholz at approximately 09:00 hrs yesterday morning. The RTR Battlegroup counterattacked late yesterday afternoon but were unable to destroy the bridgehead. The enemy were able to reinforce and break out not long after midnight. Their leading tank regiment is currently heading west along the E30 on an axis Peine-Lehre-Hannover.

Friendly forces. 22 Brigade is setting up a blocking position west of Peine to stop any enemy advance before it reaches Hannover. The RTR Battlegroup is currently attempting to slow the enemy advance but their casualties have been heavy."

Duncan cocked an eyebrow at Neil who caught his eye and sighed.

"Okay. They've had the shit kicked out of them. There's no way they'll slow Ivan down."

He looked down at his notepad.

"Mission. Along with the Dragoon Guards' Battlegroup we are to mount a counterattack against the leading elements of 10th Guards Tank Division and halt their advance.

Execution. We will cross the Mittelland Canal at Peine and attack north into the flank of the leading tank regiment which we believe is the 103rd Tank Regiment. The Dragoon Guards' Battlegroup will also attack on our left flank. It's also planned that Soviet follow-up forces will be attacked from the north by elements of 11th Panzergrenadier Division. More detailed information will be provided later as it becomes available."

Neil paused and looked around at each NCO in turn, aware of the sketchy nature of some elements of the briefing. "Any questions?"

There were several clarifications required before Neil wrapped up the briefing and the section commanders went to brief their men. All around the Company hide weary men began to prepare to go into action again.

As happens frequently in war, circumstances can change with great rapidity. The leading Soviet tank regiment suddenly swung south, back towards the Mittelland Canal. After a short, but bloody, action against German Territorial troops the Russians seized a crossing over the canal at Woltdorf.

This caused consternation at NORTHAG HQ. It was no longer an attempt to outflank 1st Armoured Division or threaten the major communications node of Hannover. It was now a serious threat to one of 1st Armoured Division's three brigades. There was significant danger of 12 Armoured Brigade being trapped against the Salzgitter Branch Canal and destroyed, leaving a gap torn in NATO lines which could be exploited by the Soviet 2nd echelon army. Even now the next echelon's 20th Guards Army was moving towards the front, ready to flood through any gap created by 3rd Shock Army.

The need for an immediate counterattack by 7 Armoured Brigade became even more urgent. The two Battlegroups tasked to carry out the attack were ordered to move immediately and NATO air assets were tasked with destroying the crossing point. Elements of I (GE) Corps to the north continued to counterattack against the Soviet divisions' trailing armoured and supply units but, despite causing casualties to men and material, the leading units ploughed on.

Chapter 13

The sound of heavy fighting drifted from the northeast where the Dragoon Guards' Battlegroup blocked the advance of 10th Guards Tank Division at the town of Siersse. From their concealed positions Lieutenant Neil's Platoon watched a pair of Lynx anti-tank helicopters head northwards flying nap-of-the-earth. Overhead RAF Harriers tore through the summer sky, heading for Waltorf and the canal crossings where Soviet reinforcements poured across to the south bank.

Colonel Masters' Battlegroup had been split into two Squadron/Company Groups, one southwest and one east of Siersse. While the leading Soviet elements were blocked by the Battlegroup in Siersse, creating an encounter battle, enemy doctrine was to keep the British pinned by fire from the leading troops while follow-on forces outflanked the defenders. The two elements of the second Battlegroup were positioned to ambush and destroy any out flanking forces before counterattacking and driving back the Russians.

Sergeant Duncan appeared as the Company's vehicles started their engines simultaneously. Exhaust smoke hung in the warm air as the sound of diesels throbbed under the trees.

"Right, lads. Mount up. They're on their way."

The infantrymen scrambled aboard their AFVs and settled in, waiting to move as reports came in from the Scimitars of the recce detachment. An enemy tank battalion had been spotted to the northeast moving to encircle the British forces in Siersse.

Corporal Norman scanned his frontal arc as the Platoon moved forward out of the trees looking for the first sight of the enemy. He also anxiously searched the sky just above the treetops, watching for enemy helicopter gunships. Beneath him the Warrior rocked at speed, the suspension soaking up the jolts caused by the uneven terrain.

Several of the tank squadron's Challengers, overwatching the advancing members of their troops, opened fire with their 120mm cannon. 1000 metres away a T-80 burst into flames as an APFSDS round smashed into the side of its hull. Two more halted with smoke pouring from their engine decks.

In the turret of Victor Three One, Sergeant Turner laid the gun on a second target.

"Target right!"

Trooper Cox stared through his sight trying to identify the target amongst the smoke and dust kicked up by the Soviet tank company. Despite all his best efforts he was unable to spot the target.

"Target not identified!"

Turner fine-layed the gun onto the T-80 he had spotted, hull down near his first victim.

"Fin, tank, on! Have you got him Mickey?"

"On!" Cox took control of the gun and concentrated on the target.

"Loaded!"

"Fire!"

"Lasing!" Cox fired the laser as the T-80 fired at a target somewhere to Victor Three One's left.

"Firing now!" Cox and Turner both watched the tracer in the base of the round fly towards the Russian tank. It impacted on the T-80 with a blinding flash followed seconds later by a rush of flame which blew open the turret hatches.

"Target!"

"Target stop!"

"Loaded!" Trooper Brinkworth had loaded another Fin round into the breech and was already cradling another in his arms ready to load again.

Turner scanned for more targets but all the Russian vehicles appeared to be burning. He opened the heavy hatch above his head and poked his head out of the cupola. In the distance burning and halted Russian tanks were partially visible through the smoke. Looking around he saw two of the Squadron's Challengers had been hit.

One of the tank's crew was gathered round their vehicle, it looked as if they were extracting a wounded crew member from the turret. The other vehicle was blazing furiously, flames rushing twenty feet into the air from the turret hatches like a blowtorch as the ammunition propellant burned and smoke poured from the engine compartment and gun muzzle. There was no sign of its crew.

"Two of ours are hit," he informed his crew. "One's Four Two, not sure who the other is."

"Everybody get out all right, Geordie?" asked Brinkworth, popping his head out of the loader's hatch. One of his drinking mates crewed Four Two.

"Somebody's hit in Four Two. Don't know who or how bad. The other one's brewed. Doesn't look like they got out … "

Turner was interrupted by tank cannon to their left rear. Brinkworth immediately dropped out of sight into the turret. Turner twisted in the cupola and looked over the rear of the turret and the engine deck. He saw 1 Troop, echeloned to their left rear, engaging targets to their front. He quickly glanced left.

"Oh, fuck!" He dropped into the turret pulling the hatch closed behind him. Grabbing the gun override control he slewed the turret left to where the second Soviet tank company was thundering towards their flank. "Target left!"

The massive turret swung smoothly to the left until the commander's sight was lined up on a T-80.

"Fin, tank, on!"

"Loaded!" Brinkworth was very glad he had already reloaded the 120mm gun.

81

"On!" Cox was sweating as he laid the aiming mark on the T-80 rolling towards them.

"Fire!" Grant, spin us left! Now!"

In the driver's compartment, Trooper Grant, ignorant of the details of the situation due to his limited vision but aware that things had suddenly gotten "interesting", turned the massive hull of the Challenger so that the heavily armoured glacis plate faced the enemy instead of the thinner side armour.

"Lasing!" The second it took the computer to calculate the correct elevation and aim off and drive up the gun on to the target seemed like a lifetime to Cox. It was only later that he realised that it could have been. "Firing now!"

The tungsten dart hit the front of the T-80's turret with a blinding flash. The enemy tank slowed as it was rocked back by the impact but continued to advance.

"Target!"

Turner watched the failure to penetrate the enemy tank with a touch of dismay. "Target go on!" He tried to appear calm as the tension mounted even more.

Cox quickly ran through his firing drill. "Firing now!"

Again an armour-piercing round sped towards the enemy. It struck as the T-80 slowed to fire and the tank shuddered to a stop. Turner watched it for several seconds but it only sat there, smoking, until the driver's hatch burst open and the bloodied driver baled out, tumbling down the glacis and huddling by the tracks desperately seeking cover.

"Target stop!"

Turner scanned for another target. It appeared that several of the T-80s were knocked out and the remainder divided between 1 Troop on their flank and 3 and 4 Troops who had wheeled left and were engaging them from the front. Even as he watched, one of 1Troop's tanks was hit and its crew scrambled clear, at least one of them seeming to be hit as they raced to safety.

It was only now, once the immediate danger had been dealt with, that Turner realised there had been no orders from Lieutenant Thomas, the Troop leader. Fearing the worst he quickly scanned the area either side of his vehicle. To his right the third tank in the Troop, Three Two, had followed his lead and turned to engage the enemy. On the left his Troop leader's tank, Three Zero, was only now pulling into place on the line.

"Victor Three Zero, this is Victor Three One. Everything okay, over?"

"Victor Three One, Victor Three Zero. All good … out."

Turner frowned at the hesitancy in Thomas' voice. The Lieutenant was fairly new and was lacking in confidence. He was often slow to pick up on, and act on, fast-moving events. In peacetime there would be time to build up his confidence and teach him the art of decision making. However, in actual combat time was a luxury they did not have. Turner suspected that the Lieutenant's luck was going to run out sooner rather than later. It was only a pity the he might take a good crew with him.

Eventually the surviving Russian tanks began to withdraw making smoke. They were attempting to draw the NATO armoured Squadron on to the battalion's third company which had taken up a defensive position along with a company of Motor Rifle troops. Behind them the NATO tanks followed up eagerly closely followed in turn by the infantry company in their Warriors.

The T-80s were shrouded in smoke, only the flash of their main guns occasionally visible in the white fog. The Challengers switched to their thermal sights and continued to score hits. Suddenly they were hit by a volley of armour-piercing rounds from the hull-down third Russian tank company. Two of the Challengers were halted after being hit.

83

Lacking Thermal Imagers the following Warriors were having difficulty spotting the enemy. Corporal Norman desperately searched his front, looking for the enemy as the vehicle rolled forward at speed. In the passenger compartment the rest of No. 1 Section were crammed together, lurching against one another with the violent rocking of the vehicle.

The motion of the speeding vehicle, along with the tension and fear generated by the impending action, was having an effect on several of the troops. Private Lister had gone pale and was fighting to keep his stomach contents down. His attempts had not gone unnoticed by Lance Corporal Davis who sat opposite him and who would be first in line for being vomited over. Lister clapped his hand over his mouth with a horrified expression on his face as his stomach lost the battle.

"Don't you fucking dare!" shouted Davis as both Privates Clark and Waters tried to lean away from Lister and any splatter. "Use your helmet!"

Clark quickly dragged Lister's helmet off and shoved it in his lap where he retched the contents of his stomach into it.

"Aw, fuck's sake!" The rest of the Section looked on in disgust, several of them feeling their own stomachs protest as the smell of vomit hit them. Both Clark and Waters leaned away as far as the cramped compartment would let them from Lister and his helmet contents. Davis rubbed his forehead with his hand, his face a mixture of disgust and relief that Lister had managed not to vomit in his lap. Lister stared back at him miserably, not even comforted by Sinclair's cheery, "Ach, better oot than in, eh?"

The passengers were rocked sideways as the Warrior braked suddenly, the bow dipping and the rear elevating before dropping sickeningly and rocking the suspension. Above them the Rarden cannon in the turret fired a three-round burst before the vehicle lurched forward again and built up speed.

"Target, BMP!" Norman spotted the turret of a BMP as it fired an AT-5 Spandrel anti-tank missile, the backblast giving away its position.

"On!" Private Taylor had the Soviet IFV firmly in his sights.

"Driver, halt!"

Once again Hubbard stamped on the brake and the vehicle rocked to a halt.

"Firing now!" This time the three-round burst was on target. Taylor watched the impacts on the BMP's turret, the enemy gunner manning the anti-tank missile mounted on the top of the turret thrown backwards by steel splinters. Smoke seeped from the turret hatch past his body.

As soon as Taylor had fired, Hubbard had accelerated again towards the enemy. Norman was trying to identify enemy positions as the fighting grew fiercer. Tank rounds, cannon shells and LAW missiles filled the air and vehicles were hit and left wrecked and burning.

An RPG round flew past the rear of the Warrior and hammered into the slab of add-on armour on the side of No. 3 Section's vehicle. The armour buckled around the impact point but the jet of molten metal failed to pierce the IFV's passenger compartment and the Warrior continued to advance, the troops inside shaken but uninjured.

Norman spotted the backblast from the RPG and caught a glimpse of other Russian riflemen nearby.

"Target!" One o'clock! Infantry!"

The Warrior's turret swung right as Taylor searched for the target.

"Taylor … one hundred metres … bushes!"

"On!"

"Co-ax … fire!"

Taylor switched to the co-axial chain gun and fired a short burst, the tracer showing that the rounds had flown wide due to the pitching of the vehicle. Another burst hammered out, this time coming close enough to force the enemy infantry to take cover.

"Hello Hotel One One, this is Hotel One Zero, over."

"Hotel One One, go ahead, over."

Hotel One Zero. Dismount the Section and deal with those infantry you were targeting. Out."

"Hotel One One. Wilco. Out."

Norman reached back and down to slide the mesh screen on the turret cage to one side and looked into the passenger compartment.

"Frame, the Lieutenant wants the Section to dismount and take out some infantry!" he shouted over the noise of the engine and the hammering of the chain gun. "There's about six of them and an RPG in some bushes at one o'clock!"

He turned back and keyed the microphone. "Driver, right."

Hubbard steered the Warrior to the right, towards the enemy targets. Norman waited until the vehicle pointed towards where the Russian infantry were concealed. "Driver, ok." The vehicle straightened and thundered towards the enemy infantry who had taken an unhealthy interest in the Warrior.

"Taylor, brass 'em up a bit more."

Once again the bursts of 7.62mm rounds caused the enemy to duck down as the Warrior roared closer. Norman lowered his head again and shouted into the passenger compartment. "Thirty metres at twelve o'clock! Taylor's got them suppressed!" He keyed the microphone. "Driver, halt!"

Hubbard stamped on the brake and the Warrior pitched forward and rocked back. As the vehicle's rear crashed back down, Corporal Frame hit the large red button above his head beside the rear door. The door sprung open, he pushed it fully open as he leapt out and the rest of the Section scrambled out behind him. As he stumbled through the hatch Lister swung his helmet, splattering its contents over the rear track before jamming it back on his head with a pained look on his face.

Frame led his Fire Team round the left side of the Warrior while the vehicle's co-axial chain gun covered them with burst of fire, keeping the enemy's heads down. As the Team went prone to engage the Soviet infantry, a burst of fire came from hidden enemy troops on their left flank. Frame went down under the impact of several rounds beside the Warrior's wheels.

The remainder of Fire Team Charlie opened fire on their original targets. Jordan fired measured bursts from his Light Support Weapon, a heavier barrelled support version of the standard SA80 and easier to handle in this situation than his usual GPMG. Sinclair fired a short burst from his rifle before settling down to fire single, aimed shots. On the far side of the Warrior, Lance Corporal Davis' Fire Team Delta also laid down suppressive fire awaiting Frame's order to assault the enemy position.

Sinclair was also awaiting Frame's orders to the other Fire Team and when they failed to come he looked around for the Corporal. Spotting the figure sprawled beside the vehicle he alerted the others.

"Corporal's down! Corporal's down!"

Hearing this Davis took over. "Sinclair! Jordan! Keep their heads down while Delta assaults!"

"Okay!"

"Delta Fire Team, prepare to move … move!"

Davis led his Fire Team in a slight arc to the right to avoid masking the other Team's fire and also that of the Warrior. The new angle gave him a better view of the enemy. There appeared to be five of them, huddled in a ditch behind some bushes. At least two of them were either dead or wounded, one of them the RPG operator. The others could only huddle against the side of the ditch as rounds cracked overhead and thumped into the ground around them. Further back, in a slight dip in the ground, unnoticed until now, stood their BMP, apparently abandoned.

Private Clark lobbed a grenade towards the ditch and the movement attracted the attention of one of the Russians. His return burst of fire caught Clark as the Fire Team prepared to rush in. The grenade detonated and Davis led his Team forward. Several short bursts from their weapons and it was over.

The other Fire Team was still under sporadic fire from their left. Sinclair and Jordan were now returning fire as their Warrior reversed into better cover. Taylor then joined in with the vehicle's 30mm cannon. After several minutes of this the enemy fire subsided.

By now the whole area was obscured by smoke from burning vehicles. In the immediate area around the Section were two destroyed BMPs, a blazing T-80 and a disabled Challenger. Nearby another two Challengers continued firing at retreating Russian vehicles and another two of the Platoon's Warriors were approaching.

One of the Warrior's opened fire with its chain gun on the area Corporal Norman's Warrior had been firing at. The vehicle braked to a halt and No. 2 Section rushed out and assaulted the enemy infantry. A quick dash forward, a few shots and they returned to the Warrior, shoving two prisoners in front of them.

The second Warrior approached and halted behind Norman's vehicle. The rear door opened and Lieutenant Neil emerged along with Private Robinson, his radio operator, and Sergeant Duncan. They jogged over to where Lance Corporal Davis, Sinclair and Jordan were kneeling beside Frame's body. Further away the rest of Fire Team Delta were giving first aid to Private Clark.

Sinclair looked up as they approached, caught Neil's eye and shook his head. Neil glanced at the body and turned to Davis. "Number One Section's yours now, Corporal." He nodded at Sinclair. "You've got the Fire Team, put up a tape when you get the chance."

Both men nodded back, "Sir."

Jordan and Sinclair bent down to remove Frame's webbing and fit his bayonet to his rifle, thrust it into the ground and hung his helmet on the butt. They then covered his body with his poncho and rejoined the rest of the Section beside the wounded Clark. Sergeant Duncan was giving out instructions.

"Take Clark over there," he pointed back the way they had come. "Number Three Section's Wagon was knocked out. There's three wounded and Linton's dead. There should be an armoured ambulance there soon if it's not there already."

He watched dispassionately as Lister and Waters carried their burden away, Clark moaning at each jolt. Watching him, Sinclair wondered what was going through his mind. On the surface he appeared to be all business and Sinclair wondered how he could do it. He shot a glance at the poncho-covered body then looked at Davis who almost seemed to puff himself up. He felt some of his own confidence leave him at the thought of Davis in charge of the Section. He also missed the thoughtful look that Duncan gave to Frame's body before becoming all business again.

" Corp'rl Davis! Get your Section reorganised. Move it!"

Sergeant Duncan also had misgivings about the new Section commander, particularly his temperament and "man management" skills. Davis was an efficient enough NCO but a bit full of own importance and had too much liking for throwing his weight about. *Anyway*, thought Duncan. *Time will tell. He may not live long enough to annoy everyone.*

"Once we've reorganised we'll likely move out to better positions. I imagine Ivan'll be back." Leaving them with that happy thought, Duncan walked back to where the Lieutenant was reporting the Platoon's status to the Officer Commanding C Company, Major Clipsom.

The counterstroke by 7 Armoured Brigade succeeded in halting the advance of 10th Guards Tank Division. Its ability to resume its advance was crippled by counterattacks on the Division's supply tail, mostly by elements of 11th Panzergrenadier Division of the German I Corps north of the British sector. By the time they were in a position to consider continuing the assault, 10th Guards' operations had been overtaken by events as fighting had all but ceased between NATO and the Soviets as the Stavka ordered a cessation of operations. An uneasy calm fell on the frontline across Germany.

Part 3

"Operation Zhukov II"

18th - 20th July 1992.

"So the important thing in a military operation is victory, not persistence." Sun Tzu.

"If at first you don't succeed, get a bigger hammer." Alan Lewis

Chapter 14

By late on 16th July, fighting had died away along the whole length of the Front. From Hamburg in the north to Bamberg in the south the guns fell silent. NATO was unclear on what was happening but was glad of the pause, taking the opportunity to reorganise and resupply. Overnight on 16th/17th July NATO units brought up supplies of fuel, ammunition and reinforcements and frantically tried to repair as much heavy equipment as possible. Units, their personnel exhausted by four days of high-intensity warfare, were able to snatch some much-needed rest.

The pause in offensive action lasted for almost 24 hours as the Soviets reviewed the situation. Diplomatic negotiations, which had been suspended once hostilities commenced, were resumed at the UN. However, very little progress was made as the German government dug in its heels as the "injured party". Apart from that the negotiations on the Soviet part were more to delay rather than find a solution.

It was clear to the Stavka, the Russian High Command, that Operation Zhukov had, while not being a complete failure, limited success. In the north 2nd Guards Army had failed in its attempt to surround Hamburg but had pushed Dutch forces beyond the city and cut Hamburg off from the south. On the North German Plain 3rd Shock Army had failed to break through the British and Belgians but 10th Guards Tank Division's limited breakthrough had compromised British I Corps' defensive line along the Salzgitter Branch Canal and forced the British to give up the ground between the IGB and Salzgitter. The Belgians had also been driven back as far as Gottingen.

In the SOUTHAG area 8th Guards Army had been halted well short of its first objective, the River Rhine, but had hit the Corps' boundary between III (GE) and V (US) Corps and made good progress before being halted. Further south 1st Guards Tank Army and 6th Combined Arms Army had greater success. 1st GTA reached its objective at Würzburg and 6th CAA had reached Bamberg and was able to partially block II (GE) Corps from attacking north into the flank of 1st GTA although they failed to reach Heidelberg and completely block the Germans' route north.

West of Peine, FRG, 09:00 hrs, 17th July.

7 Platoon's NCOs were gathered round Lieutenant Neil's Warrior as he passed on what he knew of the current situation.

"Ivan appears to have halted all operations, there's been no movement since the early hours of the morning. Word from Division is that there's no formal ceasefire but that negotiations have begun again at the UN. Whatever's going on we're glad of the break, it gives us the chance to reorganise and get ourselves sorted out."

"Any word of replacements, Sir? We're six men down in the Platoon and the Wagons need some tender love and care," enquired Sergeant Duncan.

"There'll be replacements here soon, Sergeant. 'B' Echelon will be sending Battlefield Casualty Replacements forward at some point this morning. Mostly Reservists, I think. The REME are working on the

92

Wagons and the tankies are waiting for replacement tanks from the Delivery Squadron.

There's an 'O' Group scheduled for 10:00 hrs so hopefully we'll have more after it. In the meantime get everything sorted, stock up on ammo and LAWs, get any routine maintenance of the Wagons done and be ready to move at short notice." He stood up and dismissed them. "Right, carry on."

Duncan made his way through the Company hide, checking how the Platoon was holding up. Number Three Section was understrength after losing four of its members, the remaining six badly shaken by their close call and the death of their driver. Duncan spent several minutes chivvying them until they temporarily forgot their troubles in their irritation with him. The sound of their grumbling followed him as he walked away and he felt he had done something useful.

Number Two Section was in much better spirits having escaped unscathed. Duncan was pleased to see that Corporal Evans was keeping them busy and their minds occupied. He left them much easier in his mind.

Number One Section was the one that worried him most. Corporal Frame had been popular as well as a good section commander and the very suddenness of his death had stunned his men. There was also an underlying resentment of the new commander, Corporal Davis. Davis had never been popular. Although a competent soldier, he was inclined to be officious, winding up men just as efficient as himself unnecessarily. His obvious ambition and his propensity to try and impress his superiors had earned him his nickname of "Brownie" for the alleged colour of his nose.

His obvious satisfaction at his promotion and his seeming to regard the death of Frame as an opportunity for himself had disgusted the rest of his Section. Although not unaware of his unpopularity, Davis, in his arrogance, put it down to jealousy and made no attempt to motivate his Section, preferring to drive them instead. As a result the men were working in silence, even the usually cheerful Hubbard, who was inclined to whistle or hum to himself under his breath while he worked, was quiet as he tensioned the Warrior's tracks.

Well, that's a bad sign, thought Duncan. *If Smiler's not a happy bunny things must be bad.*

He found Davis sitting with his back to one of the wheels "supervising" Jordan and Sinclair making up 200 round belts of 7.62mm machine gun ammunition and field-stripping the GPMG. He was occasionally offering the odd "helpful" suggestion. Duncan watched him for several seconds, thinking of the best way to approach the situation. *Subtle would be best*, he thought, *at least this time*.

"Corporal," he inclined his head further into the wood.

"Sergeant," Davis scrambled up and followed him.

Duncan wandered away from the activity in the Platoon area to a quiet spot. "How's the Section doing?" He asked.

"They're okay, Sergeant."

"They seemed a bit quiet there. Not like them."

Davis shrugged, "I suppose."

"Losing Frame hit them hard. You need to keep them on the ball." Duncan wasn't sure subtle was working.

"I'll keep 'em busy. Too busy to mope about feeling sorry for themselves. I'll get 'em to buck their ideas up."

So much for subtle, thought Duncan, *time for Plan B*.

"Try providing some leadership, then. Try leading instead of pushing." Duncan tried to keep the annoyance out of his voice … and failed. Try and gee them up a bit, they need to be on form for what's coming."

"Yes, Sergeant." Davis sounded dubious and slightly, but only slightly, deflated.

Duncan studied him for several seconds as Davis grew more uncomfortable under his stare. He sighed and jerked his head in the direction of Number One Section and watched Davis walk away. He let out a deep breath and shook his head. *More fuckin' problems*, he thought. *As if the Russkies weren't enough, I've got Corporal fuckin' Davis.*

Still shaking his head he walked away to check if the ammunition replenishment had arrived.

It was not only NATO that was taking advantage of the pause in operations. The Stavka had debated the situation for most of 17th July and eventually come to a consensus which it presented to the Council of Defence. The Stavka's plan was approved but with reservations, particularly fears over escalating the fighting.

Despite the risk of escalation, it was decided to continue operations against Germany and NATO. A last attempt would be made to take vital objectives for use at the negotiating table. However, if the objectives were "not secured" (use of the word "failed" was deliberately avoided. Failure was not a concept that was tolerated amongst senior officers in the Soviet armed forces … it tended to have fatal consequences for those unfortunate enough to suffer from it) then the Soviet and Polish forces would withdraw and claim that they had "punished" the Germans enough for their actions against Poland.

Further assaults on Hamburg were planned, along with a secondary attack towards Bremen to cut off the main US supply port of Bremerhaven and also I (NL) Corps. The drive on Frankfurt would be resumed as would the attempt to encircle the Ruhr. In addition a new front would be opened by an assault on Norway to deny NATO the use of Norwegian airfields for direct attacks on northern Russian airfields and to secure them for their own use for airstrikes against NATO carrier groups operating off Norway.

Already "Mission Creep" was taking effect. A limited operation with defined objectives and timescale had already began to expand into a wider war.

95

In preparation for the 2nd phase of operations the Soviets had brought forward fresh 2nd Echelon forces. In the British sector 3rd Shock Army had shifted southwards with the battered 10th Guards Tank Division spread thin between Salzgitter and the edge of the Harz Mountains at Seesen covering the bulk of 1st and 4th Armoured Divisions. The other three tank divisions were massed in the western Harz Mountains between Goslar and Osterode preparing for a dash for the River Weser along the boundary between I (BR) and I (BE) Corps.

North of the Mittelland Canal the 2nd Echelon 20th Guards Army was preparing for a thrust on Hannover and, if possible, a further advance to Minden. Using the Mittelland Canal as flank protection, once past Minden and through the barrier of the Teutoburger Wald there was a good road network to carry them on to the Ruhr.

North of Peine, FRG, 23:30 hrs, 17th July.

Once again, the newly-promoted, Sergeant Eldon was lying in a darkened hide, soaking from the drizzle and feeling particularly miserable. Behind the camouflaged observation post, further in the wood and heavily camouflaged, stood his Scimitar. Inside November One One Alpha Trooper Grainger sat dry and reasonably snug, dozing in his gunner's seat as Trooper Sanderson snored in the driver's compartment.

Eldon was still commanding the reconnaissance troop, casualties amongst the Corps' two recce regiments had been heavy and trained reservists hard to come by. Replacements were on their way but in the meantime the reinforced, but still understrength, troop was under Eldon's tender care.

From the dripping hide, using a pair of night-vision goggles he had "acquired" from a careless artillery observer who had foolishly left them temporarily unattended, Eldon could observe both the westbound E30 Highway and the western suburbs of the town of

Peine. At least he could see them in between the rain showers which played havoc with the goggles.

Earlier in the day he had watched large numbers of refugees streaming westwards along the E30 and the road which ran along the edge of the wood concealing his troop. Further east, nearer the IGB, there had been very few civilians in evidence, most having evacuated in the period of tension between the German-Polish fighting beginning and the Soviet invasion. The misery, despair and suppressed panic was obvious even at a distance as the hundreds of people drove, rode and walked towards where they thought was safety. Eldon had felt saddened by it all, surprised by the emotion. He had thought that the past week had knocked all the emotion, apart from fear, out of him.

Soon, but not soon enough for the wet, miserable Eldon, Trooper Grainger appeared to take over the observation duties. Eagerly Eldon made his way back to the vehicle and dragged his damp, weary body into the turret. He gladly accepted the mug of hot tea brewed by Sanderson using the vehicle's Boiling Vessel. Drinking it quickly and gratefully he tried to get comfortable in the gunner's seat and dropped into a fitful sleep.

He was woken abruptly by the thundering detonations of a massive Soviet barrage as the second phase of Operation Zhukov began.

7 Armoured Brigade had been pulled from divisional reserve to cover the northern sector of 1st Armoured Division's area north of the Mittelland Canal. The full weight of the fresh 20th Guards Army, advancing on a one-divisional frontage, fell on the Brigade. The lead Soviet unit, 25th Tank Division, battered the Dragoon Guards' Battlegroup aside before it could recover from the hammering of the preparatory barrage and rolled west along the E30 followed by the 32nd Guards Tank Division, 35th Motor Rifle Division and 9th Guards Tank Division.

Elsewhere in the sector covered by the British Corps the damaged divisions of 3rd Shock Army were also on the move. 7th Guards Tank Division kept the bulk of 1st Armoured Division occupied by small-scale attacks which pushed it back beyond the E45. To its south, 47th Guards Tank Division attempted to pin 4th Armoured Division in place while 12th Guards Tank Division assaulted and broke through Belgian lines north of Gottingen. The northern tank regiment of the division brushing aside elements of 4th Armoured Division's southernmost brigade, 19 Infantry Brigade.

But it was the thrust by 20th Guards Army which was causing consternation at NATO Headquarters, the first major breakthrough by Soviet forces. Suddenly there was a hole in NATO lines being exploited by four Soviet divisions with another potential breakthrough further south. Three NATO Corps, I British, I Belgian and I German were in danger of being dislocated, potentially resulting in the collapse of NORTHAG.

Chapter 15

Lt-Colonel Masters' Battlegroup had been rushed out of reserve to try and slow the advance of 25th Tank Division. 7 Armoured Brigade had been forced south of the E30 by the advance of 20th Guards Army and its other two Battlegroups were moving towards Hannover in the hope of counterattacking the Soviet thrust from the south.

The E30 Autobahn ran through woods on the eastern outskirts of Lehrte before skirting the town itself. Despite being an obvious choke point, it was hoped that the Russian spearhead was moving too fast to waste time deploying and that it would attempt to force its way through any resistance using speed as its main weapon. Any attempt to slow the Soviet advance by whittling down the leading units was considered worthwhile at this point.

7 Platoon occupied a village northeast of Lehrte itself. No. 1 Section was dug in on the southern edge of the village looking towards a road junction where several roads joined the E30. Air activity had been heavy over the area and an air battle had been observed just after daylight with several, unknown, aircraft shot down.

Corporal Davis looked round as Private Hughes, the Platoon runner, knelt behind his trench.

"The Lieutenant says they're coming, Corpr'l."

"Right, Hughes." Davis raised his voice. "Stand to! Stand to!"

Beside him the other occupant of the trench, Private Lynch, the reservist sent to the Section as a replacement, nervously picked up his rifle which had been lying on the parapet of the trench. Davis looked at him coldly

"Ready?"

"Yes, Corporal," Lynch nodded uncertainly.

"I hope so," Davis turned away and began scanning his arc. Lynch stared to his front and towards the Autobahn, looking for the first sight of the enemy.

Sinclair and Jordan were again sharing a trench. Sinclair's Carl Gustav MAW was lying within reach, propped against the side wall of the position, but as commander of a Fire Team his main job was to direct the fire of his men rather than get bogged down in tank-hunting. As always he was nervous until the action actually started. Beside him Jordan seemed his normal self, whistling softly as he scanned his arc.

"Movement! Four hundred metres, 11 o' clock, where the road leaves the treeline! Possible vehicle!" Jordan thought it was an enemy reconnaissance vehicle but hadn't got a proper view of it due to a slight mist caused by the warming morning air on ground dampened by the night's rain.

"Hold your fire, just observe!" Davis shouted unnecessarily before reporting the sighting to the Platoon commander.

The vague shape sat on the edge of the small wood for several minutes before moving into the open and revealing itself as a BRDM 2 scout car. It quickly accelerated, heading for the cover of the trees outside Lehrte. Behind it a second BRDM, unseen by the watchers, covered it from an overwatch position in the treeline.

The scout car halted just inside the opposite treeline and tucked itself into the undergrowth. After a short time one of the crew dismounted and cautiously made his way on foot further into the wood. In the meantime the second BRDM crossed to the wood and halted a short distance from the first vehicle. The commander of the second vehicle dismounted and sprinted across to the first vehicle.

A short time later the crewmember returned from his foot reconnaissance and a short discussion took place between the two vehicle commanders. The route the E30 took through the wood and past Lehrte must have looked particularly uninviting to the Russians as the dismounted commander ran back to his vehicle and the BRDM made its way northwards along the edge of the trees towards the village occupied by 7 Platoon. The original leading vehicle followed at a distance. It appeared they were searching for an alternative route bypassing Lehrte.

Jordan tracked the BRDM with his GPMG, watching it with anticipation. The whole Section was concentrating on the two vehicles, looking for any sign that they had spotted any of the British units concealed nearby. But the BRDMs continued their cautious advance without any indication that they had spotted anything out of the ordinary.

The BRDMs' advance ended abruptly as the leading vehicle ran into a hastily-laid minefield covering an area between the wood and a side road which led northwest from 7 Platoon's village. The mine detonation wrecked the scout car and left it burning. No-one got out. As the smoke of the explosion died away a Challenger belonging to 3 Troop of the RTR's A Squadron, hidden in a wood further north, fired on, and destroyed, the second BRDM.

It was some time before the next enemy vehicles appeared. The Advance Guard of the leading tank regiment was preceded by a combat reconnaissance patrol of several BRDMs. The leading vehicle halted in undergrowth south of the Autobahn, its commander watching the columns of smoke from the burning scout cars rise over the trees to his north.

After a short time one of the other BRDMs moved forwards, leapfrogging the leading vehicle, moving towards a cluster of light industrial buildings on the outskirts of Lehrte. Unfortunately for its crew the buildings were occupied by C Company's 9 Platoon who opened fire when spotted by the Russians. After a short firefight a LAW ended the argument in favour of 9 Platoon. A wounded Russian survivor was pulled clear of the wrecked BRDM by two British infantrymen.

While the Soviet reconnaissance units were held up by Masters' Battlegroup some of the Brigade's rear-echelon units had time to get out of the way of the Soviet advance. The delay allowed a REME workshop, which had set up in a service station off the Autobahn on the western outskirts of Lehrte, to pack up and retreat westwards.

101

They had even been able to gather enough heavy transport to remove vehicles capable of being repaired. Attrition amongst AFVs had already reached levels where any vehicles capable of being repaired had to be saved at all costs.

The approach of the Forward Security element of the Russian tank battalion heralded an escalation in the action. The tank company, reinforced by a Motor Rifle platoon, swung south off the E30 and advanced towards the southern outskirts of Lehrte. As swinging north of the town would take them into contact with the enemy forces that had destroyed the reconnaissance patrol, they hoped that there was a route past the defenders to the south. Unfortunately for them, waiting for them there was B Company Group which included two tank troops.

As the Russians crossed a side road running northeast to connect with the main highway they were engaged by the tanks of A Squadron's 4 Troop. The first salvo left three T-64s halted in the fields and the remaining vehicles veering to their right to take cover between two light industrial areas. This manoeuvre led them directly into a scatterable minefield covered by two Milan launchers and A Squadron's 1 Troop.

Two tanks and a BMP were disabled by the mines and subsequently destroyed by 1 Troop's Challengers. The remaining two BMPs and five T-64s ploughed through the minefield and attempted to close with the enemy but lost another two tanks to the Milans. The survivors made smoke and pulled back into the cluster of industrial buildings to their north. This led them into 9 Platoon's defensive position.

Once in amongst the buildings the BMPs halted and dismounted their infantry who immediately came under small arms fire from the British infantry. A confused, close-range, firefight commenced, leading to hand-to-hand fighting as the surviving Russian infantry gained the cover of the buildings.

One of the BMPs quickly succumbed to a LAW round but the second used its 73mm gun to blow its surviving dismounts into one of the buildings. At the same time the surviving three T-64s, badly disadvantaged in the close confines of the built-up area, desperately tried to avoid the infantry tank-hunting teams. They were trapped between staying in cover and being destroyed by hand-held anti-tank weapons and breaking out, escaping the infantry but exposing themselves to the fire of the Challenger troop.

One by one they succumbed to small groups of infantry armed with LAWs, destroying the tanks with volleys of two or three 66mm rockets. The surviving crew members were rounded up along with several surviving Motor Riflemen. Both the prisoners and the wounded of both sides were evacuated as soon as possible as the Battlegroup waited for the Soviets next move.

Sinclair was sitting in the muddy bottom of the trench, wedged in the corner, dozing with his poncho draped over him against the drizzle. Jordan kept watch, his eyes continually scanning for any sight of the enemy. Jordan suddenly flinched and dropped into the bottom of the trench and Sinclair started bolt upright as the air was filled with the shriek of incoming artillery fire.

Now wide awake, Sinclair huddled against the side wall of the trench as an artillery battalion systematically flattened the woods along the sides of the E30 before the detonations crept westwards into the outskirts of Lehrte itself. He realised that he was watching the Soviet sledgehammer in action. There would be no outflanking of the British position, no manoeuvring. They had delayed the Soviet advance for three hours but now they were preparing the way for the leading tank regiment. They were going to batter their way through the blocking force using firepower and sheer weight of numbers to break through, roll over the defenders and continue the advance westwards to Hannover and beyond.

Sinclair tore his eyes away from the sight of debris, the remains of Lehrte's eastern suburbs, being hurled through a maelstrom of artillery shells and joined Jordan in searching for the leading Russian tanks. They were concentrating so hard that Sinclair failed to notice the Platoon runner arriving at Corporal Davis' trench.

"Sinclair!" Davis was irritated that it took two attempts to attract the other Fire Team leader's attention. "Time to go! RV at the wagon!"

Sinclair scrambled out of the trench and Jordan handed his Carl Gustav up to him before scrambling out himself. Sinclair ran across to the other trench where the other two members of his Fire Team were climbing out.

"Hurry up, boys! Back to the wagon, we're pulling out!"

The trio joined the rest of the Platoon clattering through the streets to where the Platoon's Warriors were concealed. Sergeant Duncan was checking as each section reported in and piled aboard their vehicles. As the Platoon pulled out of the village the Milan detachment's FV432 rolled past and the vehicles bypassed the minefield as 8 Platoon's vehicles exited the woods and followed them.

Once the infantry element of the Combat Team was on its way the two tank troops pulled out of their positions and followed them' leaving the recce section to bring up the rear. To the south the other Combat Team was also pulling out and C Squadron Group was exiting the western edge of Lehrte. The Battlegroup was heading south to rendezvous and be re-tasked. Having delayed the Soviet advance there was no point in lingering and taking unnecessary losses trying to stop the oncoming juggernaut.

In one of the clusters of industrial buildings south of the town, two of the Battlegroup's Scimitar reconnaissance vehicles were preparing to follow the rest of their Combat Team. Sergeant Mitcham was observing the Autobahn, a last scan before pulling out. Movement where the highway left the woods caught his eye. As he watched, first one. Then three, then a full company of Russian tanks flooded out of cover and shook themselves out into attack formation heading for Lehrte. Behind them came a second company. However, it was a pair of Hind attack helicopters following the lead tank company which worried him most.

"Hello, X-Ray Two One Bravo. This is X-Ray Two One Alpha. Time to go. Watch out for the Hinds. Move now. Out."

"X-Ray Two One Bravo. Wilco. Out"

The other Scimitar reversed from its concealment and headed south, keeping the buildings between it and the enemy. Once it reached a suitable covering position Mitcham gave the enemy a last glance, seeing more enemy armour moving west, and ordered his driver to move out. The last elements of the Battlegroup headed southwards as Soviet armour poured westwards behind them.

Chapter 16

South of Hannover, FRG, 14:00 hrs, 18th July.

Colonel Masters' Battlegroup had crossed the Mittelland Canal south of Sehnde, once again moving south. Corporal Norman had guided Hubbard onto the Medium Girder Bridge erected by the Divisional engineers. On the approach to the bridge itself they had to avoid several burning vehicles, the victims of the latest air attack. Behind them smoke rose from various points in Sehnde itself where German Territorials skirmished with Russian reconnaissance forces scouting for possible crossing points and watching the retreating British.

As the last of the Battlegroup's vehicles cleared the crossing point the engineers began to dismantle the bridge. Resources like this were becoming too scarce to be demolished if they could be recovered. As the main Russian thrust was to the north it was considered worth the risk to recover the bridge.

Eventually the Battlegroup took up reserve positions west of the River Leine. To the east the two forward brigades of 1st Armoured Division were falling back towards Hildesheim, not so much under pressure from the battered 7th Guards Tank Division, which could only follow up and mount small probing attacks, but more apprehensive of the advance of 20th Guards Army. This advance had already outflanked the Division's defence line on the Salzgitter Branch Canal and now threatened the fallback position on the Hildesheim Branch Canal.

C Company was frantically performing maintenance on its surviving vehicles in a company hide. The Battlegroup's REME detachment was working around the clock ensuring that the vehicles were at least fit to travel, anything else was secondary to making sure that the vehicles were mobile. At an Order Group the Company commander, Major Clipsom, was explaining the urgent reason for this to his platoon commanders. Immediately after the 'O' Group Lt Neil called a briefing of the whole platoon.

The weary troops gathered round Neil's Warrior, the Platoon's NCOs sitting nearest the officer with notebooks and pencils ready, the rest of the Platoon sitting or reclining on the ground and leaning against tree trunks. Neil ran his hand over his face, grubby with day-old camo cream, and through his hair, matted and sweaty from his helmet, and began the briefing.

"Right, listen in, we don't have much time." He tiredly rubbed his forehead as he paused to gather his thoughts. Corporal Hastie glanced at Sergeant Duncan and raised an eyebrow as he waited for the officer to continue. Duncan gave a small shrug and patiently waited for Neil to continue.

"Things are not going well further north. Ivan is still heading west along the E30 with all four divisions of 20th Guards Army. This is a major breakthrough and it's threatening the whole Division. We're going to have to fall back to avoid being outflanked at some point soon. In the meantime we're hoping German I Corps to our north can counterattack and halt 20th Guards Army," he paused for a second, "or at least slow them down."

"In case we need to move out sharpish the REME boys are working to get as many wagons as possible fit to move. While they're doing that we need to pack as much fuel and ammo as possible and make sure all essential maintenance is done. Being able to move takes priority over being able to fight, understand?"

He paused and looked around, waiting until he got nods in return.

"We need to be ready to move out at a moment's notice if it becomes necessary. Any questions?"

There were only shaken heads.

"Right then, carry on. Sergeant Duncan, wait behind."

He discussed further details with Duncan as the Platoon dispersed to carry on the work at hand. All around the work of preparing the vehicles went on.

NORTHAG HQ, FRG, 21:00 hrs, 18th July.

The maps at NORTHAG Headquarters told their own story of how the fighting was progressing in NATO's Northern Army Group area of responsibility. Red arrows had now almost reached Hannover in the British sector and another red arrow to the south showed where a division of 3rd Shock Army had broken through the Belgians north of Gottingen and was now swinging northwest towards the River Weser. Further north spearheads reached westwards around Hamburg and Polish forces were heading towards Bremen.

General Turnbull's staff was issuing orders to commit III (US) Corps, NORTHAG's main reserve, against the Polish thrust on Bremen and elements of I (GE) and I (BE) Corps to counterattack 20th Guards and 3rd Shock Armies. Turnbull and Hardt were studying the latest dispositions, Hardt indicating the latest updates from the Intelligence staff. Hardt was thinking aloud, a habit which had manifested itself over the last few days. It helped his thought processes but occasionally irritated Turnbull by interrupting his.

"... the Dutch 1st Mechanised Division has been pushed back towards Barmstedt by the 21st Motor Rifle Division. Dutch casualties are acceptable but the Russians' have been substantial as far as we can tell.

The Polish tank division leading their 2nd Army is making progress between Soltau and Bad Fallingbostel. 1st Panzer Division was tasked to engage its southern flank but has been unable to disengage any units due to attacks by a Polish Motor Rifle division.

The British 1st Armoured Division is still engaged with 7th Guards Tank Division but they believe these are just diversionary attacks to prevent it moving against 20th Guards Army but they're being tied up anyway. Their reserve brigade is reorganising so the division is understrength. The 4th Armoured Division is holding its own against 47th Guards Tank Division but 12th Guards Tank Division's advance in the Belgian sector is threatening to turn their right flank.

The Belgians are preparing a counterattack but only the 1st Mechanised Division is available. Their other Division, 16th Mechanised, has been requested to counterattack 8th Guards Army's thrust towards the Ruhr by CENTAG. We might have given them the British 33 Armoured Brigade to help in the Belgian sector but we'll need the whole of 3rd Armoured Division to stop 20th Guards Army."

"What about 3rd Shock Army's fourth division? What's it doing?"

"So far as we know it's still in reserve. It was cut up pretty badly after crossing the canal. Intelligence indicates it's reorganising."

Turnbull placed a finger on the map north of Bremen. "I've ordered the US 2nd Armored Division to block the Polish advance towards Bremen. I didn't want to use III Corps yet, I was keeping them for a major counterattack but Bremerhaven is one of the main ports for American supplies and we have to keep the route south from there open."

He switched his attention back to the area around Hamburg. "I'm not happy about the situation there," he said, pointing to Hamburg.

Hardt looked uncomfortable. "It ... ah ... looks likely that 2nd Guards Army will reach the Elbe estuary. It's possible that the Dutch, or at least some of their forces, and Hamburg may be cut off ... temporarily."

Turnbull gave him a flat look. "Temporarily?"

Hardt shrugged. "It's unlikely that the Dutch can hold them at this time but the Russians will only have one division south of the Elbe so it will be overstretched and vulnerable to counterattacks. North of

Hamburg we have Danish forces we could use to protect the city. And of course we have that 'special reserve' in the city itself ... "Hardt smiled and paused as Turnbull nodded thoughtfully. "Which leaves us with the bigger problem."

Turnbull sighed, "20th Guards Army."

"*Ja.* The airforce is hammering them and 11th Panzergrenadiers are preparing to counterattack but at the moment the only thing slowing them up is a few small-scale attacks by Bundeswehr local Territorial units ... and they are not slowing them much. To be quite frank, it's a serious breakthrough which is outflanking both I German and I British Corps."

"The British Corps' reserve, 3rd Armoured Division?"

"A warning order has been issued."

"I'm reluctant to commit them at this point, but ... We have to commit the whole division rather than the brigades piecemeal. 24 Airmobile Brigade?"

"On standby to move."

Turnbull nodded. "Good." He perched on the corner of the table that served as his desk and folded his arms. "Anything I should know about further south?"

"It looks as if there's been a breakthrough between the Belgians and III German Corps. 8th Guards Army broke through the Corps' boundary while III Corps was busy to the south with Polish 3rd Army. It looks like becoming serious. That's why CENTAG have requested we use the Belgian 16th Mechanised Division to counterattack the thrust from the north. Only 5th Panzer Division is available to the south and the Soviets have almost a free run right to the Ruhr. I expect they'll bring French forces forward to try and block them but it'll take time and Ivan might win the race.

Around Frankfurt the situation is more fluid. The Polish 3rd Army is making gains but the Germans, Americans and the Canadian Brigade are counterattacking. The French II Corps is moving forward in the Mainz area to take up blocking positions.

In the far south 1st Guards Tank Army has been halted and both VII US Corps and II German Corps are counterattacking both 1st Guards Army and 6th Combined Arms Army. That's it so far, Sir."

"Thanks, Franz."

Both men fell silent, each lost in their own thoughts. Staring pensively at the situation map, watching the red arrows move inexorably west.

North of Hannover, FRG, 23:00 hrs, 18th July.

Feldwebel Lange lay under the dripping foliage which lined the embankment along this stretch of the E30. He tried to ignore the drizzle which was gradually soaking through his uniform. He was chilled, wet and worried as he waited for the first of the advancing Russian tanks to appear.

Further east, where his platoon commander had carried out an anti-tank ambush around the Heidehaus junction, the sounds of fighting had died away. No further word had come from Leutnant Neumann and Lange doubted there ever would. How successful the Territorial detachment had been was unknown.

Once the ambush had been sprung, Lange's two sections had destroyed the Soviet reconnaissance element that had reached his position. A BRDM scout car and a BRM sat on the autobahn, the flames engulfing them spluttering in the light rain. Several bodies lay around them, prisoners were a distraction he could not afford, he no longer had men spare to guard them.

He was aware that the attacks and ambushes on the 25th Tank Division by his Jager battalion were only pinpricks. Although the Soviets were suffering a steady drain of casualties, both in men and vehicles, the advance was still continuing at a steady pace. Casualties among the Territorial units of 62 Brigade were also substantial and there was a feeling that they were being bled dry for very little return. There was much speculation amongst the German troops as to where the British had gone. Units of 1st Armoured Division were conspicuously absent even though the Soviet advance was in the British area of responsibility. The speculation was becoming more bitter as time went by.

While glad to be hitting back at the enemy invaders the company was not convinced that their efforts was the best way to slow, or even halt, the Russians. Both Lange and his platoon commander had been convinced that destroying the major junction at Heidehaus would have created a better delay. Unfortunately there was neither the time nor the amount of demolition charges available to prepare the junction for destruction. Leutnant Neumann's casual comment that a fractional kiloton suitcase nuke could do the job better and quicker was met by a frosty stare from the company commander. Privately Lange thought the idea, joke or not, had merit. The very fact that he could actually consider such action objectively chilled Lange far more than the rain. Six days of war had already changed him and not for the better.

Gradually the growl of tank engines became audible. Lange peered through the night vision goggles but they were almost useless without any ambient light. In the darkness under the rain clouds there was virtually no illumination to be enhanced. Lange strained his eyes but was unable to discern much although he thought he could detect movement.

"*Feldwebel*, I have them. Two tanks with other vehicles behind. I can't make them out."

The Milan operator beside Lange had the advantage of the thermal-imaging sight for the anti-tank launcher.

"Ready!" shouted Lange. He knew that their advantage would only last for the first few shots. After that someone would use flares, either the enemy wanting to blind the Germans' night-vision devices and aid their targeting or the Germans themselves to allow them to see targets for their hand-held Panzerfaust LAWs.

The growl of the enemy vehicles' engines changed tone as the advancing Russians slowed as they approached their smouldering reconnaissance screen.

"Ready?" asked Lange.

"Ready," replied the Milan operator.

Lange tapped him on the shoulder with the flat of his hand and the missile leapt from the launcher and flew towards the left-hand tank. It was closely followed by another two missiles. Immediately the Soviet vehicles opened up with machine gun fire, raking the bushes and small trees lining the highway embankments.

The detonation of the first missile lit up the night as the tank was hit, followed closely by two other vehicles bursting into flames. The surviving Russian tank fired its main gun and the anti-tank round tore through the undergrowth uncomfortably close to Lange and the Milan team. Unsure if it was aimed or a lucky guess Lange and the missile team decided to move before the T-64 reloaded with a HEAT round which would be much more effective against infantry.

The movement attracted enemy fire and proved fatal for the man carrying the Milan reloads. Lange and the operator made it further into cover as the first flare burst overhead. Two more Milan missiles were in the air but the sudden burst of light flared out the operators' thermal imaging sight and both missiles missed their targets. However, their detonations did cause casualties amongst the Russian infantry who were in the process of disembarking from their BMPs

A brisk firefight now commenced as Motor Riflemen skirmished forward towards the Territorials' ambush position. Several of the German infantry fired Panzerfausts at the BMPs which were moving forwards slowly to support the infantry. One was hit and halted but the firers paid the price for their attempt and went down under a storm of small arms fire. Although the Germans were causing casualties, their limited numbers and the weight of enemy fire was reducing their effectiveness rapidly. Lange considered that they had done as much damage as they were likely to do and it was time to go.

As the Soviet flare died away leaving the scene illuminated only by the light of burning vehicles and muzzle flashes, Lange fired the coloured flare to signal the withdrawal. Covered by two machine guns, the ambushers began to withdraw up the embankment. As the Germans neared the top they were illuminated by another Russian flare and lashed with small arms and cannon fire.

Most of the withdrawing troops were hit before they could gain the embankment's far slope. Lange was hit by several rounds as he crested the slope and rolled into the darkness, unconscious and dying. The few survivors of his detachment made their escape through the allotments behind the embankment to lose themselves in the built-up area beyond.

Behind them the Russians mopped up the machine gunners and any wounded near the highway before the burning wrecks were bulldozed aside, the infantry climbed aboard their BMPs and the advance resumed. Both sides were being bled by numerous small-scale actions like this but, for the moment at least, momentum was still with the Soviets.

Chapter 17

North of Springe, FRG, 15:00 hrs, 19th July.

Corporal Norman continuously scanned the sky nervously. He was beginning to miss the low clouds and rain of the last couple of days. It had kept the Russian air force, if not away at least down to a manageable level. Now, however, they were back with a vengeance. Three air attacks in the last hour.

The Battlegroup, along with the rest of the Brigade, had been moving west. A "tactical withdrawal" … at speed. No, call it what it was, a retreat. There was very little panic but a definite sense of urgency. The Brigade, in fact the whole Division, was heading somewhere in a hurry and that somewhere was the west bank of the River Weser.

The full severity of the situation was not apparent to the British troops on the ground. They were aware of the breakthrough to the north but were not fully aware that a whole Soviet Army was powering westwards along the line of the Mittelland Canal. The earlier breakthrough of 3rd Shock Army's 10th Guards Tank Division had weakened the 1st Armoured Division's reserve brigade, 7 Armoured, and, sensing weakness, the Soviets had concentrated 20th Guards Army for a punch through NATO lines.

That punch had succeeded beyond the Soviets' expectations and the four divisions advancing on a one-division frontage had built up an almost unstoppable momentum. At this point NATO had very little immediately available to throw against it. To the south the reduced 7th Guards Tank Division was still able to pin the other two brigades of 1st Armoured Division in place east of Hildesheim. To the north I German Corps was tied up by elements of Polish 2nd Army although

11th Panzergrenadier Division was commencing counterattacks against the trailing divisions of 20th Guards Army. It was too little, too late.

I British Corps' reserve, 3rd Armoured Division, was being committed to mount a counterstroke west of Hannover and 2nd Infantry Division was forming a blocking position but it all took time. Currently the whole of I British Corps was in danger of being outflanked.

To make matters worse, in the southern half of the British sector, another pincer was forming. While another division of 3rd Shock Army occupied 4th Armoured Division, one of the Russian Army's other tank divisions had brushed aside Belgian forces and penetrated the boundary between the British and Belgians Corps. Despite counterattacks by the Belgians the Soviets had crossed the River Leine and were beginning to swing northwest towards Hameln, threatening not only an outflanking manoeuvre but an encirclement.

As a result of this the British appeared to be forced to give up all the area east of the Leine. Privately NORTHAG HQ was worried that the fallback may not end there and may have to continue beyond the Weser. This would mean the loss of a large chunk of German territory and threaten important British supply dumps along the Weser. In the past, in a major Warsaw Pact attack, the loss of the Weser line was one of the possible triggers for a nuclear response. This was developing into a major crisis for NATO.

The large roof hatch on the Warrior clanged open and Private Waters appeared in the gap, bracing himself against the jolting of the vehicle.

"Another pair of eyes!" he shouted above the engine noise as Norman twisted round towards him. He pointed upwards to emphasise the point before scanning the skies as an air sentry.

Further along the road Hubbard slowed the vehicle and skirted around a burning APC. Several casualties had been dragged to the roadside verge and the crew of a medical Landrover were treating two wounded men beside a badly damaged house. Another two wrecked vehicles sat smoking further along the road which skirted a village, the victims of a strafing run by Russian aircraft.

The Platoon was barely speeding up again when a warning came over the radio.

"Air Warning Red! Air Warning Red!"

Norman waved to attract Waters' attention, tapped the side of his helmet over his headset and jabbed his finger skywards. Waters nodded and shouted a warning down into the passenger compartment. Neither men heard the detonation of the ground-attack aircraft's ordnance but both glimpsed the SU25 as it exited the battle area at low level, pursued by a storm of machine gun fire from every vehicle within range and solitary Javelin SAM ... which missed.

After another hour a Military Policeman waved the Platoon off the road and into a wood where they joined the rest of the Company. Hubbard parked up near Lieutenant Neil's Warrior and halted. He switched off the engine and slumped in his seat, too tired to climb out of his hatch straight away. The rear doors opened and the Section slowly climbed out, stiff and sore after hours crammed in the cramped compartment along with all their gear and supplies.

Corporal Davis paused only to bark orders before leaving to report to the Platoon commander.

"Get yourselves sorted while I find the Lieutenant. Come on, move it!"

The men were too tired to even complain behind his back, only Jordan had the energy to raise two fingers. Norman slumped in his turret for a moment watching the Section stretching cramped muscles and pacing round the vehicle. He climbed from his hatch and wearily held out a hand to help Hubbard from the driver's position.

"Right, lads. Check the gear, secure anything that needs it and repack the stores. Once we know what we need I'll find the CQMS and get us resupplied. Waters, see if you can scare up some fuel. Lister, get a brew on." Norman turned to Hubbard and Taylor and shrugged. "Let's see to the Wagon. Her Ladyship requires a makeover."

Hubbard began checking the tracks and running gear as Taylor climbed back into the turret and commenced to strip and clean the co-axial chain gun. Norman watched the Section working away for a moment then decided it would be a good time for a shovel recce. He unclipped the shovel from the vehicle and set off to find a comfortable bush.

Sergeant Duncan returned along with Corporal Davis just as Lister emerged from the Warrior with the first of the tea.

"Ah, well done, Lister," Duncan said, relieving him of one of the cups. "Perfect timing."

Lister gave him a dirty look as he handed the remaining brew to Corporal Norman and turned back into the vehicle to the boiling vessel.

"Where's mine?" asked Davis.

"Ask Sarn't Duncan," came the muffled reply.

"Hurry up with the brew, then," grumped Davis as Sergeant Duncan sipped his tea with a contented smile on his face.

"What's the latest, Sergeant?" asked Norman.

"Confused. Nobody knows what the fuck is going on. The breakthrough north of Hannover hasn't been stopped and there seems to be something going on to the south with the Belgies. All that's certain is that we're giving up a helluva lot of ground. There's talk of a counterattack but it's all a bit hazy."

The rest of the Section had stopped working and drifted over to listen to the conversation in the hope of learning something about what was happening. Lister was handing out cups of steaming hot tea as Davis watched, itching to exert his authority but not wanting to interrupt Duncan.

"The Boss is off to an 'O' Group, "Duncan continued. "So hopefully we'll know more soon." He drained the last of his tea and handed the water bottle cup back to Lister. "We won't be here long so make the most of it. Get the Wagon sorted, there might not be much warning of a move."

Davis waited until he was out of earshot before asserting his authority.

"Right you lot. Back to work sharpish. C'mon, move it!"

Jordan and Sinclair looked at one another and Jordan curled his fingers and waggled his wrist while mouthing, *Wanker.* Sinclair snorted and turned back to work. Hubbard shook his head and began humming to himself as he tensioned the tracks. Jordan stood for a second watching Davis' back with a small smile on his face, he was happily thinking of ways he could shoot Davis and blame the Russians.

Half an hour later they were on the move again, heading for the River Weser.

The column was halted at a crossroads by Bundeswehr Military Police. As all those standing in their hatches anxiously scanned the skies for enemy aircraft, a column of Challengers crossed their path heading north. Those paying attention noted that the vehicles, although travel-stained, were fresher looking than their own vehicles which were festooned with stores, badly-packed camouflage netting and tarpaulins. Compared to themselves the other vehicles looked more spruce ... yet untested.

Unknown to them these were units of 3rd Armoured Division, the Corps' reserve, being brought into action for the first time to counterattack 20th Guards Army. They were heading for a position east of Minden from where they would be able to assault the flank of the advancing Soviets, hopefully after they had been blocked by elements of 2nd Infantry Division.

"Ooh, shiny!" Sinclair was on aircraft watch, leaning on the lip of the roof hatch. "Look, Norman. "Real sojers!" He pointed at an infantry company mounted in Warriors whose immaculately stored vehicles were rolling past.

Norman grinned back at him. "That's what you should look like. All squared away you scruffy little man. Scruffy and idle, that's you, that is."

Sinclair laughed as the last of the vehicles passed and the column was waved on by the Military Policeman.

The Battlegroup continued towards the Weser through the night. Delays were caused by civilian traffic which had strayed onto routes reserved for military traffic despite the efforts of German military and civilian police. The panicked, fleeing civilians caused traffic jams and accidents. However, a car was no match for several tons of armoured vehicle and accidents tended to prove fatal for the civilians involved.

Added to this were breakdowns amongst the Battlegroup's vehicles. All the hard running was taking its toll on maintenance-heavy equipment. The exhausted REME detachment was constantly in action, making hasty repairs to keep vehicles moving and recovering those that needed more work. Every effort was made to recover as many valuable AFVs as possible.

The British forces were unable to use the bridges at Hameln as fighting was continuing in the town between the remnants of the two Soviet Air Assault battalions and local German forces. As a result they crossed an engineer bridge south Hessisch Oldendorf just after dawn on 20th July. Signs of enemy air attacks were everywhere, burnt-out aircraft wrecks, a still-smouldering Tracked Rapier anti-aircraft vehicle and further upstream the ruined bridge which carried the main road. Anti-aircraft defences were heavy in the vicinity of the bridge.

By midday the Battlegroup was dispersed south of Rinteln, resting, repairing and re-arming in preparation for defending the Weser River line. To the north the crisis facing I British Corps was reaching its climax as 20th Guards Army approached Minden.

An exhausted Sergeant Duncan was making one last walk round the Platoon before getting some long overdue sleep, checking that there were no major problems needing attention. Checking up on the lads, his lads. He was pleased with the way they had handled themselves over the past week. In fact, he was bloody proud of them.

As he approached No. 1 Section's Warrior just putting one foot in front of the other was an effort. He had never felt so weary, even his bones seemed to ache with tiredness. Only Davis, curled up inside his sleeping bag, snoring, and Hubbard, crouched beside the vehicle were in sight. As he walked up he saw Hubbard slip something inside a gash bag, rather furtively he thought.

"Where's everybody, Smiler? Thought you'd all be crashed out by now."

"Just a last check, Sarn't. Then I'm hitting the green maggot."

"No problems then?"

"None that can't wait."

Duncan looked around. "So where are they then?"

Hubbard pointed. "Corporal Norman took 'em that way about ten minutes ago. Didn't say why." Hubbard added evasively.

Duncan looked at him quizzically with a raised eyebrow.

"What about sleeping beauty here? Why isn't he away?"

Hubbard smiled at the sleeping Davis. "We didn't want to wake Brownie up."

"Aww, that's nice. Letting him have his beauty sleep."

"No," Hubbard smiled even wider. "We just didn't want to wake him up. The prick doesn't deserve it."

Duncan frowned, almost too tired to be annoyed. "That's Corporal prick to you, Private Hubbard."

"Yes, Sergeant."

"Deserve what?"

Hubbard pointed again. "Try over there. All shall be revealed."

Exasperated, yet intrigued, and far too tired to argue, Duncan walked off in the direction Hubbard had indicated. Puzzled, he noticed that there seemed to be fewer men than expected around the vehicles and most of these were asleep.

Nearing the edge of the wood he halted, spotting a large group of soldiers clustered near a camouflaged vehicle. Looking closer he saw a tattered old camouflaged net draped over an unfamiliar shape. Through holes in the netting there appeared patches of blue paint. Suddenly the shape appeared more familiar. He knew what the vehicle was now.

Well, I'll be fucked, he thought.

All sorts of security and discipline implications ran through his mind and he drew a deep breath ready to deliver a bollocking. As he did so a familiar smell filled his nostrils. He paused.

Fuck it, he thought. *I'm bloody starving.*

He strode forward purposely, heading to join the queue of filthy, worn out squaddies waiting patiently beside Wolfgang's Bratty Van.

Heavy fighting lay ahead as the British sought to block the Soviet breakthrough but for 7 Platoon their part in the war was over, at least for now. Whatever happened in the next 48 hours, they were out of it. It was some other poor bugger's turn.

Chapter 18

Unknown to Colonel Masters' Battlegroup the situation was more dangerous than they thought. In addition to the northern pincer of 20th Guards Army, to the south a division of 3rd Shock Army had crossed the Weser north of Holzminden and was advancing down the west bank of the river towards Hameln.

North of Hannover, FRG, 16:00 hrs, 19th July.

The Leopard 1 shuddered as internal explosions wracked the vehicle. Smoke poured from the gun barrel and the engine deck. Flames roared out of both turret hatches as blazing propellant incinerated its crew.

"Did you see him, Engels?" Leutnant Richter, platoon commander of the stricken tank, was searching for the missile team that fired the fatal shot.

"*Nein,*" Engels, the gunner, was glued to the sight for the main gun.

"*All Sabre callsigns, this is Sabre. Disengage and pull back two hundred metres to the last cover. Acknowledge, out.*"

"Sabre Alpha, wilco, out."

Richter ordered his driver to reverse. The vehicle had barely begun rolling backwards when a Soviet anti-tank missile flew past ten metres in front of them and detonated close to the other survivor of Richter's tank platoon. Both tanks picked up speed before swinging round and heading for the nearest cover along with several Marder IFVs.

Richter's company had been attached to a Panzergrenadier battalion and, along with some reconnaissance and anti-tank detachments, now made up *Kampfgruppe* Achmann. The Kampfgruppe was one of three which were counterattacking 20th Guards Army from German Corps sector north of the breakthrough.

The counterattack had begun well, surprising several Russian columns advancing along secondary axes of advance on the flank of the main thrust along the autobahn. The Bundeswehr troops had mauled several supply columns carrying both fuel and ammunition and prevented the vital supplies from reaching the Soviet spearhead divisions. Now, however, they had run into what appeared to be a Motor Rifle battalion which, forewarned of their approach by fleeing survivors, had dug-in around a village containing an important road junction.

The original attack, launched from the march, had been repulsed and now a deliberate assault was being prepared. Time was now the main problem as reports were received that units from the two leading tank divisions were being turned back along the line of advance to block the German attacks.

Richter stood in his turret cupola waiting for the order to advance. Nearby a group of Panzergrenadiers were gathered behind their Marder, loading up with ammunition and distributing it amongst the Section. The machine gunner stood, festooned with belts of 7.62mm link, with his MG 3 resting across his shoulder, one hand holding it by the pistol grip. Richter was reminded uncomfortably of iconic photographs of Panzergrenadiers from another war.

His musings were cut short as shells from the Kampfgruppe's supporting artillery battery howled overhead and slammed into the Russian-held village. The Panzergrenadiers climbed aboard their Marder and the order to move out sent the vehicles rolling forward.

The houses in front of them disappeared in flame and smoke, rubble and bodies being tossed in the air as the short, sharp barrage continued for several minutes before changing to white phosphorous shells, creating a smokescreen to cover the advance. Despite the concealment of the smoke, several badly-aimed missiles flashed out towards the advancing Germans. Most missed but one impacted on the front of an IFV. The rear ramp dropped and smoke poured out along with wounded and shocked Grenadiers.

A tank cannon cracked and a HEAT round exploded, silencing one of the missile teams. Co-axial machine gun fire from both Leopards and Marders lashed any piles of smoking rubble visible through the smoke. Another missile flew but faltered and crashed to the ground as the 20mm cannon of a Marder either killed its operator or forced them to throw themselves under cover.

The first of the IFVs halted on the edge of the village and their Grenadiers dismounted … into a storm of small-arms fire from the Russian survivors. Grey-uniformed figures went down but a combination of the IFVs' cannon and the main guns of the Leopards shot the Grenadiers into the built-up area.

Richter's Leopard 1, along with the rest of the tank company were standing off from the buildings picking off anti-tank missile and RPG teams. Despite them, several Marders were hit by volleys of RPG rounds and left burning as they hammered the rubble with 20mm cannon rounds.

Gradually the Panzergrenadiers gained a foothold within the shattered village itself and Richter's platoon was called forward to provide heavy fire support for the infantry.

"Engels, one hundred and fifty metres, 11 o'clock, collapsed wall, RPG team. He keeps popping up."

"Target!"

"Fire!"

The 105mm gun recoiled and the pile of rubble disappeared in a bright flash along with the RPG operator. Richter was already scanning for more targets.

As the Panzergrenadiers fought their way further into the village, Richter's platoon was ordered to enter the village in support. If you really had a need to blow an entrance into a house then a 105mm HEAT round is hard to beat. In infantry street fighting there is no such thing as overkill.

With an escort of Grenadiers to keep Soviet infantry at bay, Richter slowly guided his driver through the debris-strewn street, steering him past a pair of burning BTR wheeled APCs. Engels pumped rounds into the shattered buildings following the directions of the accompanying Grenadiers. Slowly progress was being made against the Russian battalion.

Richter's concentration was abruptly interrupted by frantic reports coming over the Company net. Russian tanks had unexpectedly appeared on the panzer company's right flank, despite the Kampfgruppe's reconnaissance screen, and were engaging the German tanks.

Quickly disengaging from the infantry fight, Richter took the two Leopards back towards the village edge. Halting within the cover of the last few wrecked and still smoking houses he weighed up the situation. There were three fresh tank casualties, the Leopards smashed and burning in the open fields beyond the edge of the village.

The surviving panzers continued to engage the advancing Soviet tanks but only two T-64s were halted spewing smoke. Even as Richter watched another Leopard was hit, the bright flash of the impact of the armour-piercing round followed by a jet of flame erupting from the commander's hatch.

"Target, tank!" Richter began to engage the enemy.

Engels first shot hit the target but it was a HEAT round, already loaded for supporting the infantry, and it was defeated by the reactive armour bricks on the target T-64.

"Load armour-piercing!" Richter urged his loader as his accompanying Leopard also began to engage.

The armoured firefight continued, joined by several Milan teams recalled from the infantry fight in the village. Eventually the Soviet tanks withdrew leaving half a dozen wrecked T-64s but the relief was only temporary, more Soviet forces were reported approaching.

With the battle for the village bogging down in a prolonged infantry slog and the tank company reduced by over a third, the order was given for the German forces to withdraw. With Kampfgruppe Achmann pulling back and resistance hardening against the other counterattacking units of 11th Panzergrenadier Division, NATO's attempt to slow down 20th Guards Army with ground forces was at an end.

Above Heitlingen, FRG, 17:00 hrs, 19th July.

The pair of RAF Harriers roared low over the German countryside attempting to pick their way through the heavy air defences set up by the advancing Soviets. Several kilometres to their north another pair of aircraft were attempting the same thing less successfully. Quadruple streams of tracer rushed upwards in the distance as ZSU 23-4s engaged the second pair.

Above the low-level ground attack aircraft a major air battle was raging as the air forces of both sides strove to gain air superiority or, at least on the NATO side, the temporary ability for ground attack aircraft to work on 20th Guards Army unmolested.

The Harriers swung south aiming for a stretch of a peripheral road parallel to the E30 Autobahn which was being used by supply convoys so they would not impede the main advance. The Autobahn, with its heavy AAA concentrations, was too dangerous for air operations, casualties amongst NATO aircraft had been too high over the main axis of advance. Only a few USAF A-10s with their 30mm rotary cannon and stand-off Maverick missiles were operating over the Autobahn and even then their loss rate was heavy.

It was also felt that hitting the supply convoys would be more effective in slowing or stopping the Soviet advance. Lack of fuel and ammunition would inevitably lead to the armoured spearhead grinding to a halt. The question was, would it happen in time to save NORTHAG from being ripped wide open.

All along the Harriers route, columns of Soviet vehicles clogged every road. To avoid the congestion on the major roads supply convoys had spread out onto the minor roads to the north of the main axis of advance despite the fact that this took them closer to NATO units threatening the flanks of the advancing Soviets.

Off to the east the pilots glimpsed the dust and smoke which marked where one of 11th Panzergrenadier Division's counterattacking *Kampfgruppen* was making progress towards the main units of 20th Guards Army. The progress of these assaults was slowing perceptively as resistance hardened and armoured units were peeled from the main advance to protect the flanks.

At regular intervals along the route they were following columns of smoke rose into the air, marking where victims of previous air attacks burned. At various distances other NATO aircraft could be glimpsed dropping their ordnance and speeding away at low-level. Streams of tracer and smoke trails from surface to air missiles crisscrossed the sky. The occasional fireball showing where an unlucky aircraft had been hit.

Following the waypoints showing on the Head-Up Display both aircraft banked and began the run in to their target, a fuel convoy attempting to find what cover and concealment they could in the streets of a sprawling village. After the turn the second aircraft banking away to achieve the separation necessary to avoid running into the detonations of the first aircraft's missiles, before turning back onto the correct course well behind the leader.

The attack would be carried out using the Harrier's unguided Matra rocket pods. After a week of high-intensity combat stocks of smart weapons were already running low and in a target-rich environment like this, unnecessary. If anything the missile spread and the concentration of vehicles in the constricted streets would make the rocket strike more effective.

Small-arms fire rose to meet the first aircraft as it sped towards the release point. Much of the heavy or dedicated AAA assets were with the armoured spearhead and there was very little left to go around for the many logistics assets. The Harriers ejected flares to decoy heat-seeking missiles as several man-portable launchers hurled their projectiles at the aircraft.

The pilot triggered the two pods and 36 rockets rippled towards the target area. Detonations ripped through the buildings as the rockets impacted and a large bubble of flame soared into the sky and spread the length of a street as a fuel tanker went up. The Harrier banked sharply and pumped out flares as it rapidly exited the target area.

The second Harrier attacked, aiming for a different area to that wreathed in smoke and blazing fuel, and its rockets turned more of the village and the supply convoy to rubble and wreckage. It also released a stream of flares to decoy the few missiles that were half-heartedly sent its way and followed the first aircraft back towards friendly airspace.

Both aircraft headed back towards their dispersal site, currently set up in a large supermarket north of Minden. The return journey was more dangerous than the outward one as the draining of adrenalin following the actual attack led to a tiredness and loss of concentration that the pilots had to fight to overcome. However, it was bad luck rather than carelessness that killed the pilot of the second aircraft of the pair.

He overflew a wood which must have been the temporary cover for a target which was thought more deserving of dedicated anti-aircraft protection. A quadruple stream of cannon tracer, fired by a ZSU 23-4 concealed at the wood's edge, hosed the air and caught the aircraft in its stream. Several 23mm rounds ripped through both the engine intake and cockpit and the Harrier flipped over and cartwheeled along the ground, shedding debris and flames before coming to rest as a scattered pile of blazing wreckage.

The surviving aircraft flew on, unaware of the loss of his wingman, back to his base. Once there he would refuel and rearm and return to carry out more airstrikes. The action would be repeated several more times during the course of the evening ... if he survived.

To the south the southern pincer of the Soviet assault was also beginning to suffer unexpected logistical difficulties from an unexpected source.

Realising the danger, 4th Armoured Division had disengaged from 47th Guards Tank Division late in the evening of 19th July and began pulling back towards the Weser. During the night of 19th/20th July the Division crossed the Weser in the area of Hoxter and Holzminden. Their withdrawal took the British troops across the lines of communication behind the main spearhead of the 12th Guards Tank Division advancing down the west bank of the Weser.

East of Holzminden, FRG, 02:00 hrs, 20th July.

The Soviet supply convoy idled at the roadside, tucked under the trees and hopefully safe from the attentions of NATO aircraft. Its commander, *Kapitan* Rostov, fumed inside his Iltis jeep, frustrated by the unexplained delay. The Traffic Regulator who had flagged down the lead vehicles had moved on before Rostov was able to question him on the reason for the halt. Rostov was now stuck, waiting for orders to move on. He was acutely aware that 12th Guards Tank Division's lead regiment was relying on the fuel sitting in the stationary tankers to continue its advance.

Exasperated by the inactivity Rostov pushed his door open and stepped out into the darkness, unsure of what he could do but preferring doing something over doing nothing. In the distance artillery rumbled but the darkness under the trees seemed full of engine noise, both far and near, which he could hear over the sound of his tankers' idling engines.

Thinking it may be another convoy moving up he closed his eyes, opened his mouth and turned his head from side to side trying to decide which direction the noise was coming from. As he listened the crack of a high-velocity cannon sounded from the front of the column. As he peered into the darkness the night was lit up by one of his vehicles turning into a fireball.

Rostov ran towards the front of the column as some of his drivers jumped down from their cabs confused as to what was happening. Others gunned their engines, preparing to try and move their vehicles out of danger.

"*Tovarich, Kapitan! Tovarich, Kapitan!*"

Soldiers attempted to question him as he ran towards the sound of firing but he ignored them.

Machine gun fire was now coming from ahead and small-arms fire from his own men had begun and was growing. As he neared the blazing tanker he saw a small tracked vehicle emerging at speed from a forestry track at the side of the road, silhouetted as it crossed the road between him and the burning tanker, and disappearing into the trees opposite. Rostov didn't know what it was but he did know it wasn't one of his,

It was followed by several boxy shapes, enemy armoured personnel carriers, firing from their cupola mounted machine guns. Muzzle flashes lit the night and tracer strips reached out, touching another tanker and spewing another bubble of flame.

Suddenly aware of how exposed he was on the road he veered off to take cover in the treeline. Around him some of his men were returning fire with their assault rifles while others were taking cover amongst the trees. In the flickering illumination of the burning vehicles and muzzle flashes Rostov struggled to identify any of his NCOs to help him bring order to the chaos.

Yet another fireball appeared at the rear of the convoy followed by the crack of heavy cannon. Rostov ran back through the trees, tripping and stumbling on fallen branches and tree roots, trying to find a spot to observe the rear of the convoy in relative safety. He halted as a huge, shadowy shape rumbled up the road towards him, tracer hosing from its turret. He was blinded and deafened as the presumed enemy tank's main gun fired and yet another of his vehicles burst into flames further along the road. He fell to his knees as the massive shape clattered past, its tracks squealing on the road surface barely feet away.

He found himself crouching in the undergrowth, stunned and rendered helpless by the sudden tide of violence that had burst out of the night. He could only watch helplessly as a stream of tanks and other, unidentified, vehicles roared past, shooting up his tanker company and leaving his unit destroyed. Without any direction his troops had ceased to fight back and the survivors, like their commander, were hunkered down in cover hoping to ride the attack out.

As a result the 48th Guards Tank Regiment would wait in vain for the fuel it needed to continue the advance.

In a series of confused night actions considerable damage and casualties were caused to the Soviet supply lines. Retreating Battlegroups overran lorry convoys carrying ammunition and fuel moving up to support the advance. The result of this was to starve the spearhead of supplies and this, along with the diversion of front-line units back along the line of advance to protect the supply lines and counterattacks on the base of the penetration by Belgian forces, seriously slowed 12th Guards Tank Division's advance until it was halted south of Hameln by the ceasefire of 21st July.

Chapter 19

On I British Corps' northern flank the combination of 11th Panzergrenadier Division's counterattacks from the north and the determined, if costly, air strikes by the RAF and other units of 2nd Allied Tactical Air Force had slowed, but not halted, 20th Guards Army's advance. This delay allowed 2nd Infantry Division to form a blocking force east of Minden.

24 Airmobile Brigade took up positions on the edge of the woods of the Schaumburger Wald, north of the Mittelland Canal, while 15 Brigade occupied a blocking position around Buckeburg plugging the gap between the Schaumburger Wald and the Buckeberge ridge. The Division's third brigade, 49 Brigade, was astride the E30 Autobahn between the Buckeberge and the River Weser at Hessich Oldendorf, blocking further progress of any Soviet units along the Autobahn.

This had forced the depleted Soviet reconnaissance units leading 20th Guards Army to look for an alternative route to the road network south of Minden which would take them to the Ruhr. The route chosen took them along Highway 65, past Stadthagen, which sat squarely between the two terrain features and led directly to the British blocking position at Buckeburg. The Soviets knew NATO forces were in the area but had little idea of their actual strength.

To complete the ambush, 3rd Armoured Division had positioned itself along the lower northern slopes of the Buckeberge ridge south of Highway 65. They were concealed and waiting for the leading Soviet divisions to advance into the killing ground.

The Schaumburger Wald, FRG, 10:00 hrs, 20th July.

Sergeant Eldon's Scimitar had withdrawn into 24 Airmobile Brigade's positions after two days of falling back in front of advancing

Soviet troops, watching, reporting on strength and direction of advance and calling down air and artillery strikes at every opportunity. Now Golf One One, along with the other surviving Scimitar of the Troop, Golf One One Charlie, was guarding the left flank of 24 Airmobile Brigade.

Eldon was trying to pick out the Milan positions of the left flank battalion. Being an Airmobile unit it possessed twice the usual number of Milan firing posts. However, the camouflage was excellent and he had only spotted two positions. He hoped the Soviets would not be as observant as him.

In the distance he could see aircraft making an attack run, RAF Harriers flying a mission against the leading Soviet troops. As he watched there was an explosion in the sky and smoking wreckage could be seen falling towards the ground. There was no sign of a parachute.

The downdraft of helicopter rotor blades lashed the trees around the vehicle. A Lynx anti-tank helicopter roared low overhead and headed southeast towards the highway. Part way there it slowed down and hovered behind a village awaiting the attack order. Further to the left another was visible as it popped up and launched a TOW missile.

"Movement, Sarge. Three thousand metres, 10 o'clock, vehicles."

Eldon trained his field glasses on the area Grainger had indicated. The slight shimmer of the heat haze made it difficult to make out details of the vehicles but Eldon knew that there were no friendly vehicles to their front. As he watched they changed formation as artillery fire began to bracket them.

As they came closer, Grainger was able to identify them as Russian tanks, whether T-64s or T-80s it was not yet clear. The nearest Milan posts had also identified them and half a dozen missiles leapt from their launchers and sped towards the approaching vehicles. Eldon tracked them into the dust and explosions that obscured the target tanks. Several vehicles were hit and halted, spewing smoke then bursts of flame.

More missiles flew towards the advancing tanks and more vehicles were hit. In the distance Eldon could see more armoured vehicles swinging south to try and avoid the British fire. More detonations bracketed them as defensive artillery fire targeted the new enemy unit. Bright flashes could be seen as anti-tank missiles found new targets. More columns of smoke rose into the sky.

Soviet artillery now began to impact on the NATO positions, starting with heavy-calibre mortar fire followed by heavier artillery from the leading tank regiment's artillery battalion. Eldon dropped into the turret and pulled the hatch closed behind him. Shrapnel rattled against the Scimitar's armour as he peered through the vision blocks trying to continue observing the progress of the enemy attacks through the dust and smoke of the barrage.

By now the first wave of Russian tanks had been halted. Half the leading battalion was stopped and burning, the survivors finding whatever cover was available and engaging the NATO defenders. While they pinned the defenders in place another battalion attempted to outflank the position to the south only to run into the brigade's second Airmobile battalion.

Again the Russian tank battalion was badly mauled by the dug-in ATGW teams. A further attack by the tank regiment's third battalion also failed with heavy casualties. At this point there was a lull as the 335th Guards Tank Regiment of the 25th Tank Division, which formed the Divisional 2nd echelon, prepared to assault the NATO blocking force. They had no intention of trying to force a crossing of the canal but to mask the units moving south to continue the advance from NATO fire.

At the same time as these preparations were taking place the Soviet Division's 175th Tank Regiment was attempting to break through 15 Brigade's blocking position at Buckeburg. Here the fighting was heavier as the Brigade's battalions only had their normal allocation of Milan firing posts. However, heavy air activity by NATO ground attack aircraft and the built-up nature of the terrain offset the disadvantages of the light infantry units against armour.

By early afternoon the two leading tank regiments had been fought to a standstill. While the Divisional 2nd echelon was preparing to mount a second attack westwards towards Minden the following tank division moved up to add its weight to the advance. 32nd Guards Tank Division swung south of Stadthagen and commenced an advance southwest along Highway 65.

Along the Buckeberge Ridge, south of Nienstadt, FRG, 15:00 hrs, 20th July.

Corporal Webb watched the Soviet reconnaissance screen working its way past Nienstadt. He was heartened to see that there were less vehicles than he would have expected, proof of the attrition the Soviet formation had suffered. As he watched, one of the BRDMs halted and began to smoke, a victim of their opposite numbers, the reconnaissance platoon supporting the Coldstream Guards' infantry Battlegroup which was dug-in between Sulbeck and the ridge where Webb's Hussars Battlegroup waited to spring their ambush.

He watched the Russian reconnaissance try to find a way past the British blocking force and fail. He watched the lead tank regiment launch a textbook hasty attack from the line of march and be repulsed. And he watched the Russian divisional artillery pound the defenders. It was only when the first tank battalion of the following tank regiment swung south of Nienstadt and commenced its assault that his radio crackled into life.

"Hallo, all November Four callsigns. This is November Four Zero. Prepare to engage, over."

"November Four Zero, this is Four Two. Roger. Out."

Webb switched to the internal intercom.

"Right, lads. Time to earn our pay. Get ready to engage, Bomber."

Trooper Harris, Four Two's gunner, shifted to a more comfortable position in his seat and began scanning for targets. Above him in the commander's seat Webb did the same. They both watched the ongoing battle between the infantry battlegroup and the Soviet tank battalion, picking their first targets.

"All November Four callsigns. This is November Four Zero. Engage now."

"Bomber, tank, on!"

"On!" Harris had the target tank. It looked like a command tank.

"Fire!"

"Lasing!" Harris concentrated on the target vehicle as the gun drove up and the ellipse in the sight surrounded the target.

"Firing now!"

Webb flinched slightly at the blinding flash of the main gun firing, as he always did no matter how much he was expecting it, and felt the 62 tonne Challenger rock backwards on its suspension. He watched the tracer in the APDSFS round fly towards its target and was rewarded by a bright flash as it struck the target T-64. The enemy tank began spewing smoke and rolled to a halt.

"Target!"

"Target stop!"

Webb was already scanning for his next target.

"Fin, tank, on!"

Once again the crew went through the firing sequence and another Soviet tank was left burning. Around them the other Challengers of Bravo, Charlie and Delta Squadrons sent round after round downrange towards the disintegrating Soviet battalion. Very little fire was coming back their way. NATO artillery fire added its destruction to that of the tank guns and counter-battery fire caught several of the Russian artillery units as they attempted to shift fire and pound the British-held ridge.

In desperation the Soviet divisional commander threw his third tank regiment, 343rd Guards, into the battle. He believed that the British blocking force was about to buckle and that he could punch through and either continue the advance or have one of the following divisions pass through and continue on beyond the Weser. Unfortunately he was out of touch with the current state of events in 20th Guards Army due to heavy radio jamming by NATO. The remaining two divisions had been brought to a halt due to counterattacks from 11th Panzergrenadier Division and heavy air attacks by 2nd Allied Tactical Air Force. Most of these attacks had fallen on support units bringing up supplies of fuel and ammunition to the front and, although the two divisions had suffered minimal casualties in their fighting units, they were almost completely immobilised due lack of fuel caused by outrunning their supply lines and attrition amongst the units trying to bring supplies forward. The only reason that the forward two divisions were still able to attack was because the bulk of their supplies had moved forward before the air and ground attacks began in earnest.

Up on the ridge Webb watched as yet another tank battalion, accompanied by a Motor Rifle battalion, assaulted the Guards' Battlegroup's positions. A second tank battalion swung towards his Battlegroup to protect against the flanking force and a third followed, waiting to exploit any gaps in the British defences. Already the trailing battalion was suffering from air attacks by Allied aircraft.

Once again the Challenger crew went through their firing drills, over and over again. Their ammunition had been topped off during one of the lulls in the Soviet assaults. This time they did not have it all their own way and several Challengers were knocked out, one of them was towed from its position by a Chieftain Armoured Recovery Vehicle and hauled back to the REME workshops.

"Hello all November Four callsigns. This is November Four Zero. Prepare to move out. We're going to advance and counterattack Ivan. We'll destroy the unit in front of us and hit the flank of the otherbattalion. Out." The Troop leader sounded keen, raring to go.

"November Four Zero, Four Two. Wilco. Out. Stocksie, get ready to move," ordered Webb as the tank rocked again under the recoil of the main gun.

In the driver's position Trooper Stocks checked his instruments and prepared to move forward. He was glad of something to do as up to now he had to sit there, powerless to do anything, while the turret crew fought the tank. All he could do was sit there, waiting for the Russian round to smash through the front armour and kill them all. Now it was his turn to perform as part of the team.

"All November Four callsigns, November Four Zero. Move now!"

"November Four Zero, November Four Two. Moving now." Webb keyed the intercom. "Stocksie, advance."

Trooper Stocks revved the engine and the huge vehicle reversed from its battle position, swung round and rolled forward down the slope towards the maelstrom of fire and burning vehicles. Around it the rest of the Battlegroup did the same. They had barely gone a few yards before a Soviet barrage crashed down around the positions they had just left.

Webb flinched as detonations rocked the vehicle and shrapnel howled off the turret armour. Within seconds the vehicle had cleared the beaten zone and run out of the barrage which continued to pound the trees behind them. Once clear of the explosions Webb opened his hatch, trading the relative safety of the turret for better observation. If they were going toe to toe with the Russians he needed to see them before they saw him, quickest on the trigger lived at these ranges.

In front of him were several burning tanks, spewing smoke and obscuring targets further away. He considered ordering Harris to switch to thermal imaging but was unsure if the number of burning vehicles would confuse the sight picture. Movement to his right attracted his attention and he caught sight of a T-64 amongst the rubble of a group of wrecked buildings as it fired. A Challenger a hundred metres to his right, busy engaging another target, was hit on the side of its turret. There was a bright flash and pieces of the storage basket and the crew's personal gear flew in all directions. The vehicle skidded to a halt and the driver bailed out as smoke poured from the turret hatches, followed a second later by a roaring pillar of flame as the main gun propellant charges ignited.

"Gunner, target right!" Webb used his gun control to lay the gun in the direction of the target. "Fin, tank, on!"

"On!" Harris had acquired the target and took control of the gun.

While this was happening, Lennon, the loader, had picked up the next round to be loaded. He had already loaded an APDSFS round and bagged charge in the breech before the tank had moved forward.

"Loaded!"

Listening in on the intercom, Stocks slammed on the brake and the massive tank rocked to a halt.

"Fire!"

"Lasing!"

"Firing now!"

As the main gun fired, Stocks revved the engine and the tank accelerated forward again. Both Webb and Harris anxiously watched the fall of shot. The round hit the rubble towards the rear of the enemy tank and it was unclear if it had been hit. Webb watched as its turret began to swing towards them.

"Target!"

"Shit! Target go on!"

Webb watched in horror as the 125mm gun on the T-64 swung towards them and commenced tracking their tank. "Fire for fuck's sake!"

The tank again rocked to a halt, just as the Russian tank fired. Webb watched in relief as the AP round flashed past in front of the Challenger, the enemy gunner confused by the last minute halt.

"Fire!"

"Firing now!"

As the Challenger pulled forward both Webb and Harris were relieved to see the round impact on the enemy tank, followed by a burst of flame and smoke.

"Target stop!"

This order spread the relief to Lennon and Stocks, neither of which could see what was happening but knew from the tension and urgency in the commander and gunners' actions that danger was close. Battle was particularly disorientating for the loader as he had no easy access to a view outside of the tank although the constant action of loading tended to keep his mind off what was happening outside ... until the actions of the commander and gunner signalled mortal danger.

As the Challenger drove through the remains of the Soviet tank battalion, Webb began hunting for new targets. Only wrecked and burning Russian vehicles met his gaze. The Battlegroup ploughed on until they could see more enemy vehicles firing towards the west, their vulnerable flanks towards the advancing Challengers.

"Target left!"

While the King's Hussars Battlegroup tore through the attacking tank battalions of 343rd Guards Tank Regiment, the Soviet reserve battalion, losing a steady drain of vehicles from air attack, began a move towards taking the attacking British Battlegroup in the flank. Concentrating on the battle in front of them they were unaware of a third British Battlegroup belonging to 4 Armoured Brigade also advancing from the Buckeberge ridge.

The Royal Hussars Battlegroup caught them strung out, heading towards the battle to the west. Within half an hour the tank regiment had been savaged and the Soviet division's advance brought to a halt. The other two brigades of 3rd Armoured Division now pulled into blocking positions to prevent the trailing two Russian divisions from continuing the assault. 20th Guards Army's breakthrough was finally halted, albeit after it had cost NATO almost all the territory east of the Weser.

By 01:00 hrs on July 21st the front in Germany had fallen eerily quiet. This did not mean that all fighting had stopped but it became clear that it appeared that Soviet forces had halted their advance and were holding in place. Both sides licked their wounds and took stock of their respective situations.

In fact this had been a political decision by the Soviets. The Stavka had argued that the momentum of the advance should be sustained but the politicians, mindful of the limited aims and timescale of the operation, argued that it was time to halt, take stock and try to bring political pressure to bear on NATO to agree to an end to the fighting on their terms. To mollify the military they proposed to move up reinforcements, partly as a threat and, if the ceasefire broke down, to resume the attack.

However, this was dependant on coming to an agreement with NATO. They expected NATO governments to be reasonable and willing to negotiate. They had failed to consider how partially occupying a country while reducing its towns and cities to rubble and killing or imprisoning its citizens would affect the "reasonableness" of an already aggressive German government.

Chapter 20

General Turnbull was briefing the senior members of his staff on the ongoing political situation.

"The cessation of offensive operations by the Soviets has now been confirmed as deliberate. The UN have confirmed that the Soviets are willing to negotiate a ceasefire. It appears they have offered to halt operations and to withdraw to the former IGB following successful negotiations regarding the situation between Germany and Poland. The terms they're looking for haven't been spelt out yet. Either that or they haven't been passed down to me." He shrugged and continued. "Anyway, apparently the Germans aren't playing ball. With thousands of their troops as POWs, the massive damage to their country and the loss of life amongst the civilian population and their military, they're getting bolshie and refuse to negotiate."

He glared at Major General Hardt who was shifting uncomfortably in his seat but who met his gaze with a determined look. As did the commander of I (GE) Corps.

"So, we'll have to take as much advantage of this pause as we can. We don't know how long it'll last. We have to reorganise, reinforce and resupply as much as possible and recover and repair as many armoured vehicles as we can. I don't think the ceasefire is going to hold much longer so let's make the most of it."

When he was left alone he glanced at the mass of reports littering his desk. He had read them all and had a good grasp of the state of his forces. *Could be better but could be a lot worse*, he thought to himself.

Turnbull studied his map which noted the dispositions of his NORTHAG forces. He saw where American and Polish forces battled to control Bremerhaven in the "Bremen Corridor", where the Danes, Germans and Dutch fought the seesaw battles around Hamburg and the Danish border and where 20th Guards and 3rd Shock Armies sat between Hameln and Minden.

The Soviets had tried to surround and destroy the British Corps and had almost succeeded. In doing so they had created a bulge in the line, a salient which could be used to propel forces towards the Ruhr. However, this may also be an opportunity for NATO.

Now was the time for NATO to counterattack on the North German Plain but the Army Group's main counterattack force, III (US) Corps, was bogged down in the "Bremen Corridor". However, the bulge, the "Hameln Salient", offered an opportunity to trap several Russian divisions and push the line back beyond Hannover with a further opportunity to swing north behind the Polish forces threatening Bremen, cutting them off and destroying them. Unfortunately the only forces available, apart from the fresh 7th Panzer Division, the German Corps' reserve, was the battered British divisions of BAOR.

The more Turnbull looked at it, the more it seemed worth the risk. NATO had to start regaining ground and pushing the Soviets back, putting itself in a better negotiating position. And it had to do it soon. He was aware of terms agreed in political circles between the belligerents regarding "limited aims" and "limited actions" and wondered, if the fighting bogged down, how long it would be before someone thought it worthwhile to use something less "limited" to gain an advantage.

There's nothing like a chemical strike or even a bucket of instant sunshine to make a hole for a breakthrough or halt a rampaging division, he thought, and shuddered. Exercises were one thing but no-one wanted to end a shooting war with the message, "you see a bright flash in the sky".

Turning his thoughts to more pressing matters he called in his planning staff to draw up a plan for a major counterattack. US forces had already begun counterattacking in a limited way in the far south around Schweinfurt and Bayreuth. It was time for NATO forces in the north to push back. Hard.

Printed in Great Britain
by Amazon